The pursuit was almost over. Ryder had launched himself at the quarry as soon as he'd gotten close enough.

The man had whirled and fired, but the shot had gone wild when Phoenix had hit him below the knees and taken a bite of his leg.

Ryder left his own gun holstered rather than chance sending a bullet into the officers still at Sophie's. He'd seen them gathering when they'd helped him locate the fleeing criminal, and knew the fence would slow them down enough that he'd have to finish this job himself.

He ducked a punch, then landed one of his own before wrapping the shooter in a bear hug and shoving him to the ground.

Phoenix immediately went for the arm holding the gun.

The wiry attacker tried to bring the muzzle to bear on the dog. Ryder was on him too fast. "Drop the gun!"

ROOKIE K-9 UNIT:
These lawmen solve the toughest cases with the help of their brave canine partners

W9-BPJ-114

Valerie Hansen was thirty when she awoke to the presence of the Lord in her life and turned to Jesus. She now lives in a renovated farmhouse in the breathtakingly beautiful Ozark Mountains of Arkansas and is privileged to share her personal faith by telling the stories of her heart for Love Inspired. Life doesn't get much better than that!

Books by Valerie Hansen

Love Inspired Suspense

Rookie K-9 Unit

Search and Rescue

Serenity, Arkansas

Her Brother's Keeper
Out of the Depths
Shadow of Turning
Nowhere to Run
No Alibi
Dangerous Legacy

The Defenders

Nightwatch
Threat of Darkness
Standing Guard
A Trace of Memory
Small Town Justice

Capitol K-9 Unit

Detecting Danger

Visit the Author Profile page at Harlequin.com for more titles.

SEARCH AND RESCUE

VALERIE HANSEN

HARLEQUIN® LOVE INSPIRED® SUSPENSE

Special thanks and acknowledgment are given to Valerie Hansen for her contribution to the Rookie K-9 Unit miniseries.

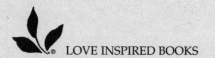

Recycling programs for this product may not exist in your area.

ISBN-13: 978-0-373-67773-3

Search and Rescue

Copyright © 2016 by Harlequin Books S.A.

www.Harlequin.com

Printed in U.S.A.

Seek and you shall find; knock and it shall be opened to you.
—Matthew 7:7

As I have continued to write book after book,
it has occurred to me that I can never fully acknowledge
all the amazing folks who have helped and encouraged me
along the way. This book is dedicated to all those
unsung heroes who are ready to share a smile or a hug
no matter what their own needs may be.

And, as always, to my Joe, who is with me in spirit.

ONE

Sophie Williams faced Desert Valley's new police chief, Ryder Hayes, with a smile, hoping he wouldn't ask what she was up to and object before she had a chance to convince him she was acting for his benefit.

Anybody would be tense about taking over as chief after Earl Jones finally retired, but Ryder had received a double whammy. He'd discovered that he'd been working beside his late wife's murderer, and the killer of others, for over five years. Former police department secretary Carrie Dunleavy had fooled everyone and had disappeared weeks ago, just as Ryder and his team had discovered she was the killer they'd been after for months. The whole town was unbelievably on edge. No wonder the new chief had been a tad short-tempered lately.

"I'm going to make a quick run to town and back," Sophie told him, noting his scowl in response.

"Be careful. You may have been a cop once," Ryder said, "but you're a dog trainer now."

That was a low blow. Sophie clenched her jaw while the chief brushed a speck of lint off his dark blue uniform and continued as if clueless. "We all have to be on guard," he said. "There's no telling where Carrie is or whether she's through killing people. There's nothing normal about Carrie. I have a feeling she's sticking close to town, watching us."

Given the shrine to Ryder that had been found in Carrie's home, Sophie had to agree. Carrie was in love with Ryder, had killed his wife, had killed two rookie K-9 officers who were like stand-ins for him. Why she'd murdered Sophie's predecessor, lead dog trainer Veronica Earnshaw or had attacked prominent resident Marian Foxcroft, no one knew yet. Until Ryder and his rookies had answers, until Carrie was behind bars, everyone had to be careful. Sophie nodded. "I'll keep my eyes open." She tossed back her shoulder-length blond hair and faced him with a determined look.

He arched a brow. "Are you carrying?"

"Of course." She patted a flat holster clipped inside the waist of her jeans and further hidden by her blue T-shirt. "I won't be out and about for long. I'm going to the train station to pick up a dog."

"Why didn't you say so in the first place?"

"Because I wanted to surprise you."

She watched Ryder stroke the broad head of the old yellow Labrador retriever at his feet. The Desert Valley K-9 training center hadn't been run-

ning regular sessions since the last rookie class
had been temporarily assigned to help in the investigation of the murders and attacks they now
knew Carrie had committed. Therefore, Ryder
was highly likely to suspect Sophie was picking
up a potential replacement dog for him.

"I don't appreciate that kind of surprise," he
said.

Sophie rebuked him gently. "Look. Poor old
Titus is more than ready for retirement. We both
know that. And your little girl will love having
him as a full-time pet. It's not as if you're aban-
doning him."

Ryder passed his hand over his short, honey-
colored hair, clearly frustrated. "Lily already plays
with Titus every night when I go home. He and I
are a team. It's as if he can read my mind. This is
not the right time to trade him for a newer model."

"Maybe it isn't for you," Sophie said. "But what
about what's best for your dog? We both know
he'd keep going until he dropped in his tracks because he's so dedicated. Is that what you want?"

"Of course not."

"Then trust me." She began to grin as she
headed for the door. "The paperwork's all taken
care of. I'll be back in a flash."

She was still smiling a few minutes later
when she parked at the small railroad station and
climbed out of her official K-9 SUV.

Dry August heat hit her in a smothering wave.

Thankfully, the scheduled train was already there so she wouldn't have to stand on the outdoor platform for long.

Sophie was always eager to get a new dog but it was not normal for her to feel this nervous. That was the chief's fault. He'd planted seeds of apprehension when he'd suggested that Carrie might still be in the vicinity, and that possibility kept Sophie from fully enjoying herself.

A sparse crowd was beginning to disembark as she approached. She shaded her eyes. *There!* A slim, young police cadet had stepped down and turned, tugging on a leash. The welcome sight brightened her mood. Grinning, she offered her hand to the courier. "Hello! I've been expecting you. I'm Sophie Williams."

"This is Phoenix," the young man said, indicating the silver, black and white Australian shepherd cowering at his feet. "I hope you have better success with him than we did."

"I've read his file." She let her free hand drop in front of the medium-size dog, ignoring him as he sniffed her fingers. As soon as the three-year-old canine began to visibly relax, she said, "You can pass me the leash now."

"I don't know, ma'am. He's pretty skittish. You sure you don't want me to walk him over to your car and crate him for you?"

"That's the last thing I want," Sophie said. "Did he give you trouble on the train?"

"Not to speak of. I kept a good tight hold. He mostly just sat on my feet and shook a lot."

She grasped the end of the leash, gave it slack and took several steps back before asking. "Is he shaking now?" The way the courier's eyes widened almost made her laugh. Instead, she politely bade him goodbye, turned and walked away with Phoenix at her side. Every maternal instinct in her was on standby, yet she knew better than to fawn over the dog too soon.

"You already have a lot in common with your new partner," Sophie said softly, watching Phoenix's ears perk up. "He's hard to get to know, too, although who can blame either of you? He lost his life's partner and, in a way, so did you when your handler died in the line of duty."

As they approached the parking lot Phoenix hung back, putting tension on the leash.

"Heel," Sophie ordered, firmly but calmly.

The dog refused to budge.

She faced him, the leash slightly loose. "What is it, boy? We were doing so well. What's scaring you?"

Phoenix was sitting with his back arched and head lowered as if trying to hide in plain sight.

The poor animal was terrified. Sophie's heart went out to him and she broke her own rule. Gathering the leash as she slowly edged closer, she dropped into a crouch so she and Phoenix were eye to eye.

A loud bang echoed fractions of a second later. Sophie recognized a rifle shot and instinctively ducked before she'd fully processed what was happening.

The already-traumatized dog surged toward her. She opened her arms to accept him just as a second shot was fired. Together they scrambled for safety behind her SUV.

She was reaching up for the door handle when a third bullet took out the windshield.

Shouting for bystanders to take cover and waving them away, Sophie drew her weapon and cocked it, prepared to defend herself—and praying she wouldn't have to.

Ryder was livid. And more afraid than he dared let on. "I *told* her to watch herself out there. Who called it in?"

"Sophie was the first. She said she was ready to return fire but never did get a bead on the shooter."

"Description?"

The dispatcher shook her head. "Some callers said it was a man and some said a woman."

Ryder rounded on the pack of rookies who had been made his temporary deputies. "Let this be a lesson to all of you. Never let your guard down. Now get your dogs and gear and let's roll." He pointed to the bloodhound's handler, James Harrison. "Especially you and Hawk. I want *evidence*."

"Yes, sir."

The chief glanced over at the whiteboard as he prepared to leave the police station. It was all there. Every victim's photo, including that of his late wife, Melanie. It didn't matter how much it hurt him to keep seeing her picture, it had to stay posted. She was an integral part of Carrie's crime spree; the beginning, the key, for the simple fact she happened to be married to him.

Ryder tore himself away and raced for his car. Enough people had already died at the hands of the madwoman who wanted him, or his blond look-alikes, to fulfill her distorted sense of romantic destiny. It must stop now. They were not going to lose one more life. Not on his watch.

Sirens howling and lights flashing, he and the others pulled out onto Desert Valley Road. Ryder floored the accelerator. Multiple incoming reports had not mentioned any victims, but he needed to see for himself. Sophie Williams might be hardheaded but she was a great dog trainer. He'd hate to lose her.

Was that the only reason his pulse was pounding? he asked himself. Probably not. It was true that all his deputies and the staff at the training center were special to him, yet he and Sophie had occasionally seemed to connect on a deeper level. Which was another strong reason for him to keep his distance. If Carrie imagined that he and Sophie were even good friends it might be enough to put the innocent trainer in the crosshairs. Which was exactly where she had ended up today.

Ryder's pulse jumped as he skidded to a stop outside the Tudor-style depot. There she was! Sophie was not only on her feet, she was pointing and apparently giving directions to other arriving officers.

Ryder hit the ground running. "Keep your head down."

"The shooter's long gone," she called back.

He stopped beside her, on high alert despite her assurances. "You okay?"

"Yeah. I hate to think what might have happened if I hadn't bent over when I did."

Ryder's jaw clenched. He started to grab her arm, then stopped himself. "Get in the car and fill me in."

"It's too hot for that."

"I'm running the auxiliary air in my unit. Come on."

"Titus is with you?"

"No. I left him in my office." When Sophie didn't move quickly he scowled. "Well?"

"Just a second. I need to coax Phoenix to come with us on his own. I don't want to muscle him into obedience."

A mottled, grayish muzzle poked from beneath the damaged SUV as Sophie spoke softly and reached out. Ryder didn't know what to say. If that sorry excuse for a K-9 cop was supposed to be his new partner, the obstinate trainer had better rethink her plans. No way was he going to accept a trembling basket case in place of a heroic partner like Titus.

The new dog slunk over to Sophie and pressed against her lower legs as she straightened. "This is Phoenix."

"Um…"

"He'll come around. He's already better than he was when he arrived. I had a courier bring him so he wouldn't be frightened by being treated like freight."

"I don't think it helped," Ryder said flatly. "If he crouched any lower he'd be crawling on his belly like a commando."

"Trust me." Sophie gave him a slight smile. "I really believe you and this dog will work out together. He needs a strong, seasoned handler like you, and you need a replacement partner."

"I need a good partner, emphasis on *good*."

"He will be. You know we don't have the funds right now to bring in a fully trained K-9, and this one deserves a second chance. If it happens he doesn't work out, we can think about pairing you with one of the younger dogs. They're just not ready yet."

"If you say so." He opened the rear door and waited until Sophie managed to load the dog, then held the passenger side for her. As she slid into the car he was struck by her courage and calm expertise despite the danger she'd just faced. That was part of the problem he had with her. She was very good and she knew it, which made her far less tractable.

Ryder smiled to himself. If she'd gotten a dog with those same tendencies she'd have been quick to send it away as a pet or maybe farm it out to the service dog program that Desert Valley Police Department rookie Ellen Foxcroft had recently started.

He could tell Sophie was studying him as he slid behind the wheel. When she asked, "Why are you grinning?" he decided to tell her.

"Just thinking. If you got a dog half as obstinate as *you* are, he'd wash out of the program in a heartbeat."

"There's a fine line between being dedicated and being foolish. I see myself as dedicated."

Although he wanted to remain aloof he couldn't help chuckling. "Dedicated to running things your way, you mean."

She shrugged, reflecting wry humor in her twinkling hazel eyes. "Hey, if my way is the best way, why not?"

Ryder sobered immediately and glared over at her. "Just make sure it doesn't get you killed."

Sophie knew she had barely cheated death at the railway depot. In order to cope and remain functional, she usually relegated troubling thoughts to a separate part of her psyche. This time, however, it was a bit harder to do. The tight expression on Ryder's face didn't help.

Sophie was half-turned in her seat, checking on the condition of the dog in the back, when the vehicle began to move. "Hey! Where are we going?"

"Away from here," he said.

"Why? I told you the danger is over. It has to be with all those K-9 rookies milling around. What did you do, bring the whole team?"

"Yes."

Viewing his profile, Sophie admired his strong jaw and muscled forearms. He was every bit a chief, in demeanor as well as appearance. The way he carried himself spoke more loudly than words, and his pristine blue uniform fit perfectly, unlike the way the previous chief's shirt had strained to stay buttoned over his ample stomach.

Ryder apparently sensed her attention because he glanced to the side. "What?"

"Nothing." Sophie was afraid she was blushing. "I was just thinking."

"About the shooter?"

"Right. The shooter. Why assume it was Carrie? I mean, would she suddenly switch to a rifle when her previous weapon of choice was a handgun?"

"Why not?" Ryder said, continuing to cruise slowly down Main, "She shot my wife and Veronica, but she pushed rookie Mike Riverton down steep stairs and burned down rookie Brian Miller's house with him in it. Carrie has no known MO when it comes to how she murders her victims."

Shivering with those memories, Sophie said, "I just can't see Carrie accurately aiming a rifle. She's too scrawny to hold it steady."

"Maybe. Maybe not. She did miss."

"Well, somebody did. Too bad it wasn't caught on surveillance cameras."

Nodding as if pondering the attack, Ryder pulled into a deserted parking lot and stopped beneath a shade tree, letting the engine idle to keep the vehicle cool. "If not Carrie, then who?"

"How should I know?" She raised both hands, palms up, and shrugged. "I was too busy taking cover to make notes. All I know is there were three shots and they all seemed to be coming from the east side of the depot building. Whoever it was took a big chance of being spotted. Somebody *must* have seen something."

"We'll sort that out back at the station after I've read the reports. That's one reason I deployed all the K-9s. We may as well make full use of them while they're still temporarily assigned here."

Sophie sighed. "I suppose so. I'll be glad to get back to running new training classes but I will miss these rookies when they move on. They've kind of grown on me."

"Me, too," Ryder admitted. "It's nice to have

more officers. Particularly when their salaries are being paid by the richest woman in town."

"Marian Foxcroft." Sophie thought of the woman who'd arranged to have the newly graduated rookies stay on to solve the murders and mysterious deaths over the past five years. Someone had attacked Marian in her own home—and that person was very likely Carrie Dunleavy. Why, was a question no one had an answer to. "I hope she recovers from her head injury, for her sake and for poor Ellen's." Sophie knew that Ellen Foxcroft, one of the rookies, hadn't been very close to her mother before the attack. Everyone was pulling for Marian. Sophie decided to change the subject. "It's nice to be able to have all the rookies' partners around for a little longer, too."

"Right. The dogs, too." He cast a quick glance over his shoulder. "Well, all except for one. What possessed you to send for—Phoenix, is it?"

"Yes. Phoenix. We have him on a trial basis, just in case he doesn't work out, but I think you're going to be surprised. Besides, he was a bargain."

Ryder arched his brows. "I don't doubt that."

"Hey, don't criticize him before you give him a chance. At one time, this dog was very good. He can be again."

"What happened to him?"

Taking a deep, calming breath Sophie explained. "He lost his partner in the line of duty. They were ambushed in an alley. Even though he was wounded, too, Phoenix stood guard over his fallen partner until reinforcements arrived."

"And after that he stayed scared?"

"Not exactly. Several other officers tried to work with him. When that failed, he was sent to rehab training in the southern part of the state, then reassigned, but he was too emotionally fragile to be of much use."

"You think you can cure him?"

"I think I understand him. That's a start." She hesitated. "Been there, done that."

Ryder was shaking his head. "So, you expect to convince a dog that the death of his handler was inevitable because that's what you've been telling yourself about the loss of your own partner, back when you wore a badge?"

Wondering if she would be able to sound logical, Sophie paused to gather herself. Her mouth was dry, her palms damp. She knew full well that her narrow focus on the criminal she and her former partner, Wes Allen, had been pursuing was what had cost him his life. Acting as his backup, she'd failed to notice a hidden gunman—until it was too late. Wes had died on the spot and it was her fault. She'd left the force shortly thereafter.

Sophie suppressed another shiver. Here in Desert Valley she had colleagues who would probably understand. One of them was sitting next to her.

Confiding the full extent of her lingering guilt and pain, however, was out of the question.

"That all happened long ago," she said. "I've found my niche training dogs for law enforcement."

"It's still excess baggage. We all carry plenty."

She could tell by the faraway look in his blue eyes that he was remembering his wife, the mother of his little girl. At least he still had Lily to give him solace. Sophie had nothing left but her work.

Pressing her lips together tightly she considered her personal life. Her best friends were dogs—and that was just the way she wanted it. People had hurt and disappointed her as far back as she could remember. Listening to her parents quarreling, she had often hidden in her room, hugging the family dog and trusting him to keep her safe. Law enforcement had seemed the perfect career choice at the outset but she had quickly realized she was not equipped to accept loss, particularly the death of her own partner. In turning to K-9 training she had, in a way, gone back to the solace she'd found as a frightened child. Not that she was about to admit it.

"I've recovered from my past," Sophie finally said. "You will, too. Just give it time."

Ryder was shaking his head. "No. I don't ever want to forget."

A sense of melancholy enfolded her. She had

never come close to finding the kind of love and devotion this man held for his late wife, nor did she ever hope to. A lifelong commitment was the kind of thing dreams were made of and she knew better than to entertain such fancies.

She had her job, her dogs and a career many people coveted. Heartfelt prayer had led her to Desert Valley and circumstances were keeping her here. That was enough. It would have to be.

A sidelong glance at Ryder convinced her further. He needed her help and that of the dog she was preparing for him. Call it a job or a ministry or whatever, it was why she was where she was at this moment in time. She would not waste the opportunity.

While it was wrong to think of hugging away his pain, it was right to support his rise in rank. Merely the fact that he had been promoted to police chief while still technically a K-9 cop was a wonder. Keeping him active and qualified with a dog for as long as he wished to be was up to her.

She closed her eyes for a moment and thought. *Father, thank You. Please stay with me.*

"You okay?" Ryder asked.

"Fine." Her voice had a catch in it the first time so she repeated, "Fine."

"Do you want me to drop you back at the training center or take you home?"

"Home, please," Sophie said. "I want Phoenix

to get used to living with his handler again. We may as well start right away."

"You won't take any unnecessary chances? Promise?"

"Cross my heart." She made the motion.

"Okay. I'll go in ahead of you and check your house."

Her "No," came easily.

"No?"

Sophie was nodding. "Thanks, but no thanks. That won't be necessary. If there's anything wrong at my place the dog will alert."

"How? By ducking and shaking the way he did at the depot?" The chief sounded cynical.

Reminded of the shooting incident and the way her own hands had trembled in its aftermath, Sophie covered her emotions by shrugging and saying, "Whatever."

To herself, she added, *That will make two of us feeling fearful.* All her previous efforts to escape the rigors and threats of active law enforcement had been rendered ineffectual the moment those shots had been fired. If she had not been going home with a dog, traumatized or not, she might have welcomed human intervention.

Ryder was adamant. "Look. Until we know whether or not the attack on you was random, I'm going to pull rank. I'm inspecting your house when we get there. Is that understood?"

Sophie was so relieved she nearly sighed aloud. Instead, she purposely pouted, scooted lower in the seat and folded her arms, making sure her courageous image remained unspoiled. "Yeah, I get it."

In truth, she was thankful. The house she'd been renting for several years sat on a double lot on East Second Street and backed up to undeveloped land, a quiet location that had seemed ideal until she'd started feeling vulnerable.

Right now, she'd have gladly settled for high stone walls instead of wire fencing, and maybe a turret with an armed guard or two, preferably one like Ryder Hayes.

If he turned up anybody hiding in her house, waiting to hurt her, she didn't know what she'd do. But she was pretty sure she knew what Ryder would do—whatever it took to see that she was taken care of.

TWO

Ryder had figured Sophie's objections to his entering her home had been based on its messy condition. One look had immediately changed his mind. She was a good housekeeper. The dishes were washed, the bed made, and a vacuum cleaner stood sentinel in a corner of the living room. There were slipcovers on her padded furniture and an extra throw on the sofa. He could understand that when a person kept bringing new dogs home.

Satisfied that she'd be fine, he divided the remainder of his day between his office and the depot crime scene. He was a methodical investigator. Usually. This time he felt as if he was missing something, some clue that would better explain why Sophie had been targeted. But what?

After being fooled so thoroughly by Carrie, he found himself mistrusting everyone, a trait which had gotten him into hot water with Sophie after her predecessor, head trainer Veronica Earnshaw, had been murdered at work. Unwarranted suspicion and hurt feelings at that time meant he'd have to be doubly sensitive about how he chose to dig deeper into Sophie's past. Looking for someone who may have held a grudge since her days as a police officer was going to be his first objective.

The most logical choice was to simply question her, although he hadn't gotten very far when he'd tried that before. There were cut-and-dried facts in her file, sure, but that wasn't the same as getting her input on old cases.

Planning to speak with her the following day, Ryder put Titus in his car and started for Lily's babysitter's house. Passing the veterinary office adjacent to the training center, he did a double take. There was only one old car he knew of that lacked a backseat and was decorated with decals of various dog breeds. Sophie Williams was out and about.

He parked at the curb. Bypassing the deserted front counter he headed down the hall to the exam rooms. Phoenix was perched on a stainless steel table while Sophie comforted him.

Her eyes widened. "Oops. Caught me."

"You *promised* me you'd stay home today."

"I believe I promised I wouldn't make any unnecessary trips." She'd looped an arm over the trembling dog's shoulders while Tanya Fowler, the veterinarian, held a stethoscope to his ribs.

"This is necessary?"

"Yes," Sophie replied.

"And why is that?"

"Well, you wouldn't want a sick dog to contaminate our working teams or facility, would you?"

He eyed the shaking canine. "He's sick?" Judging by the way Sophie's cheeks bloomed even before she answered, he doubted it.

"Um, no, Tanya says he's healthy." Sophie brightened. "But you have to agree. We did need a professional opinion."

"And now we have one. Let's go. I'll follow you home and check the place again."

"Don't be silly. There's no reason for you to go to all that trouble. I told you, I'm armed."

"A handgun is no defense against a rifle unless your attacker runs out of ammo and tries to club you with it."

The face she made at him was hilarious. Rather than smile and lose authority he turned away and pointed to the door.

Although Sophie didn't hurry, she did comply. Giving the vet a brief hug and thanking her, she lifted Phoenix down and started for the exit.

Ryder let her pass before he allowed himself to grin behind her back. Of all the trainers and handlers he'd ever known, this one was the most admirable—and the most hardheaded. She had a quick answer for everything and a dry wit that often surfaced at the most needed moments. Working in law enforcement was tough, particularly for men and women who were in it for altruistic reasons, and they often needed the kind of emotional release that laughter provided.

Sophie was out the door and halfway to her car before he stopped her. "Wait. You forgot something."

"What?"

He'd already scanned their surroundings, satisfied they were safe for the time being. "You never once checked for threats. You just barged out the door as if you were the only person in town."

"Like I keep telling you, Phoenix will let me know if there's danger."

"Sure. After he has his own nervous breakdown."

The view of Sophie, chin held high, her eyebrows arched and her hands fisted on her hips, was so cute he could hardly keep a straight face.

"I'll have you know he saved me at the depot this morning. If he hadn't held back I might not have bent over and could have been shot."

That was enough to ruin Ryder's day. "Why is this the first I'm hearing about a connection?"

She shrugged. "Actually, it just occurred to me when you questioned his abilities."

"*You* didn't hear or see anything to make you duck?"

"Nope. The first I knew I was in trouble was when the bullets started flying. Which reminds me. How long do you think my SUV will be out of service? I like my car but it lacks a certain dignity."

"If I had my way you'd be stuck in your office for the rest of the year. Or longer."

It was the rapid way Sophie's expression changed that focused his attention. She was clearly trying to maintain her bravado and failing miserably. What had he said or done to trigger such a transformation? Even shortly after the shooting that could have taken her life, she hadn't looked this doleful.

Concerned, Ryder approached. "What is it? What just happened?"

"Nothing."

He reached out, not quite touching her shoulder, and heard an unexpected growl at his feet. Wonder of wonders, the usually shy dog had stepped in front of Sophie and was prepared to defend her.

"Whoa." Ryder withdrew. "Maybe there is hope for Phoenix after all."

"There's hope for all God's creatures, given the right environment and enough love," Sophie said. "Now, if you'll excuse me, I'll be going."

She let the dog jump in before she slid behind the wheel of her decal-covered car.

Because he assumed she'd take off as fast as possible, Ryder jogged back to his idling patrol unit, unlocking the door remotely. Titus was panting but comfortably cool thanks to a special air-conditioning system that functioned whether the car was moving or not.

It was easy to follow her to the small house on

Second Street. Ryder stayed in his car and observed, just in case. The usual spring was missing from Sophie's step. She was almost plodding, as if bearing a heavy weight on those slim shoulders. Seeing such a change come over her—and linger—had him worried.

Somehow, he had caused emotional injury to someone he admired, and for the life of him he couldn't figure out what had happened. They'd been talking about her SUV and he'd made some sarcastic remark about wishing she were stuck in her office, but surely that couldn't have been enough to instantly depress her.

Puzzled, Ryder kept watching and mulling over the problem until Sophie and the dog were safely inside. Whatever he'd done had also bothered the new dog so it must be something simple. Intuitive.

"I raised my voice?" he muttered. "I was just worried about her but..." *But perceived anger had demoralized her.* Perhaps Sophie's mood had had less to do with what he'd said than it did with his forceful delivery.

So, who had verbally abused her in the past? And why were the residual effects lingering in her twenties?

A strong urge to climb out of the car and apologize was not easy to quash. Surely there would be a better time to speak with her in private and express regret. Besides, it might be too soon to approach after inadvertently hurting her.

That was what bothered him the most, even though it had been unintentional. He would never purposely harm anyone.

"Except for Carrie," Ryder murmured. It would be better for all concerned if he were not present for the capture. His respect for the law was strong, yet he didn't want to have to put it to the ultimate test.

Modern laws didn't allow "an eye for an eye" biblical justice. God forgive him, he sorely wished it did.

Before releasing Phoenix, Sophie led him on a comprehensive tour of her house, allowing him to sniff to his heart's content now that she was sure he was healthy. It was good to have a dog underfoot again, even if she was going to eventually have to relinquish him to a new partner.

She stroked the top of his head and saw his stub of a tail begin to wag. "That's right, boy. I'm one of the good guys. You can trust me. Now let's see if I can trust you."

She unsnapped the leash. At first, the timid dog stayed close to her, not venturing far until he caught a scent and put his nose to the floor.

"You have natural ability and curiosity," she said, keeping her voice gentle. "Good boy." The stubby tail wagged faster. "I can get you over your fear. I know I can."

So, who's going to help me? Sophie asked herself. It had been a long time since she'd had such a strong flashback to her dysfunctional childhood, and even longer since she'd let it show enough to be noticeable. What was the matter with her? Chief Hayes—Ryder—was liable to think she was as unstable as the new dog.

"I'm not. Not at all," she insisted. "There must be lots of people who don't like to be yelled at." And, to be totally honest, Ryder had not actually shouted. Maybe it was his reference to her being stuck in her office, combined with a harsh tone, that had pushed her panic button. As a child she'd spent long hours hiding in her closet and had even crawled under the bed a time or two, seeking escape from her parents' anger. By themselves, her mother and father were generally amiable, but put them together and they didn't seem to know a civil word.

"Which is why I love dogs," she reminded herself, smiling at her new boarder. "Come, Phoenix."

His ears perked up and he stopped to look at her. Pleased, she repeated, "Come," and turned to walk away. To her delight, the mottled gray Aussie trotted along behind. By this time his short tail was wagging his whole rear end.

"Good boy. Sit," Sophie commanded. Phoenix plunked down so fast it was a blur. She made him wait while she entered the kitchen, then released him to join her.

"You are going to be perfect for the chief," she told him. "Now, let's get you food and water bowls and fix a place for you to sleep in my room. Are you hungry?"

Two leaps and a skid on the slick, marbled vinyl floor took Phoenix straight to the refrigerator. Tongue lolling, he danced in circles.

Sophie had to laugh. She cupped his furry face on each side and gazed into his light brown eyes, positive they reflected intelligence. "Dogs eat dog food out of bowls in this house," she told him. "Didn't they teach you safety in those other places?"

He barked in her face. "Eww, dog breath," she joked. "Follow me and pay attention. Lesson one is going to keep you from getting poisoned."

Sadly, it was necessary to teach working dogs to ignore treats from strangers in order to protect them. The Canyon County Training Center did allow their graduates to eat from a human partner's hand, but only when given a specific command.

With Phoenix close at her heels, Sophie pulled out two weighted dog dishes and placed them on a mat beside the back door. The expression on his face when he saw they were empty made her laugh again. "Patience, buddy. I'm working on your dinner."

He watched her every move, quivering with excitement before she released him to eat. Then he approached his food as if he'd been starving. That kind of dog could be harder to train to leave food fragments alone but considering his rapid improvement she felt confident he was a quick learner.

As soon as he'd licked up the last crumb and polished the food dish with his tongue, Sophie accompanied him outside.

The instant his paws hit the porch, Phoenix bristled and began to growl. Sunset was casting her small backyard in long shadows, the lingering heat making portions of the ground shimmer.

Sophie followed the dog's line of sight to her chain-link fence and past it to a stand of ancient ponderosa pines. The climate might not be conducive to grass and a lot of greenery but it was perfect for drought tolerant trees and scrub brush. Normally, that kind of growth made it easier to spot threats but at this time of day every silhouette seemed to mask danger.

A gust of wind lifted her hair, bringing a welcome draft of cooler air. She squinted to see what was bothering Phoenix. If he was the kind of dog who alerted at every lizard or blowing leaf he might not be suitable after all.

Opening her mouth to speak, Sophie never had the chance. Phoenix leaped off the porch without touching the steps and tore toward the wire fence. His bark was fierce, his hackles bristling.

When she saw the problem her heart skipped

a beat. A large rattler was coiled, ready to strike, mere feet in front of the dog. If she called him now and he turned his back on the reptile he was sure to be bitten!

Although she was still armed she didn't want to shoot so close to civilization unless she had to. Praying silently, she slipped off the porch and opened the door of her metal toolshed.

A broom would only irritate the snake and a shovel was too unwieldy. A hoe, however, was ideal. If she couldn't scare off the rattler she might be able to pin its head long enough for Phoenix—and herself—to escape. It wouldn't be the first snake she'd routed since coming to Desert Valley, but it was the first incident involving a working dog. If the fangs pumped venom directly into a dog's head, the chance of survival wasn't good.

Phoenix was still barking when Sophie approached behind him. Too bad she and the Australian shepherd didn't know each other well. If they had, she would be able to better predict his reactions.

Staying to one side, Sophie inched closer. There was no way she could swing faster than a snake could strike. The trick would be getting the metal blade of the hoe between it and her dog, then trying to pin it or push it away. If it had recently fed and was only defending itself, it might turn and flee.

Another short step closer. And another. She extended the hoe. The snake's forked tongue flashed out, its mouth opening. She could see folded fangs descending. It was ready. So was she.

Phoenix backed up slightly. The rattler's head rose. Sophie was out of time and she knew it. She thrust the blade forward. Her aim was accurate. With one lunge she managed to force the viper's triangular head to the ground.

Startled, Phoenix jumped back. He began to circle her, barking, while the snake writhed, struggling to get free. As soon as she was certain the dog was out of striking distance she gave the blade a last push, dropped the handle and made a dash for the back door.

She didn't get far. A slightly smaller rattlesnake was crossing her path. Two more were curled up on her back porch! Incredulous, she climbed onto an old rickety picnic table, hoping it wouldn't collapse under her weight.

"Phoenix, come!" The order was more than forceful. It was filled with alarm.

Sophie braced herself as the dog vaulted to the bench, then joined her atop the table. Encountering one venomous snake wasn't that unusual in the desert but this… This was incredible. Why in the world had they suddenly invaded? There was no wildfire to drive them into her yard. And if there had been a den located nearby she should have noticed problems right away, not several years after moving in. Such reptile gatherings tended to be seasonal and this was her third summer here.

Wide-eyed, she scanned the ground around the table and noted three more reptiles. They instinctively knew that direct August sun would kill them and had taken refuge in shady spots. Unfortunately, some were resting between the picnic table and her kitchen door. Once night fell they'd move. But by then she'd have trouble seeing well enough to avoid being bitten, not to mention keeping Phoenix safe.

Sophie was trapped. Frustrated. Mad at herself. She hadn't even brought the hoe to the table with her. How long could she stay crouched without her legs and feet going to sleep? And how long could she keep the new dog from attacking the reptilian menace and getting himself killed?

Easing into a sitting position and preparing to fold her legs, she glanced down. One of the smaller snakes was climbing onto the bench. Once he got that far he'd be able to reach the top of the table! Sophie lowered one foot over the edge, hooked a toe under the side of the bench, and kicked.

It wobbled. Teetered. When it fell all the way onto its side it was farther away, hopefully far enough to keep all but the largest rattlers from getting to her.

And speaking of those… A triangular head poked over the edge of the table. Its forked tongue vibrated. There was no way she was going to try to kick this one away.

Drawing her gun she started to take the standard two-handed aim, then thought better of it and used one hand to grab the dog's collar so he wouldn't bolt when she fired so close to him.

The first shot hit the reptile under the chin and threw it backward. Trembling, Sophie leaned over the table's edge to make sure she'd killed it—and came face-to-face with its bigger brothers. More shots finished those. By this time, she sincerely hoped her neighbors had heard enough to call the police because she didn't want to take her eyes off the snakes for a second.

Up until then, Phoenix had held his position pretty well, considering. Now, however, he rose slowly, hackles bristling, and stared past the side yard to the street beyond. Sophie recognized the dog's attitude immediately. He was no longer concerned with chasing dangerous snakes. There was something else in his sights. Something he'd sensed was evil without even seeing it.

She swiveled, kneeling, looked in the same direction and brought the muzzle of her gun up, ready for self-defense.

A sudden thought stripped away her bravado. How many shots had she fired at the snakes? How many bullets were left? Did she have *any*? In the heat of the moment she'd failed to count and if she dropped the clip out now to look, she might not be able to replace it fast enough.

Only one thing was certain. There was at least *one* shell left in the chamber or the slide would have stayed back.

Was one shot going to be enough?

THREE

"**Y**ou'd better get over here, Chief," rookie officer Shane Weston said, once Ryder answered the phone. "And don't bring Titus. I think we've killed all the snakes but we could have missed one or two."

"That was what all the ruckus was about? There was enough radio traffic to have handled a small war. I could hardly make out a thing the way you were interrupting each other's transmissions."

"Sorry, sir. It was pretty hectic for a while. I'm surprised she managed to keep that dog safe."

Ryder scowled. "Dog? What are you talking about? Was the call at the training center?"

"No," Weston said. "I thought you knew. Sophie Williams had a backyard full of rattlers."

"What? The dispatch was for the corner of Desert Valley and Second, so I didn't realize they meant her house down the block." His pulse jumped when he imagined the scene. "I might expect a bunch of snakes gathering like that in the spring but not now. How many were there?"

"Hard to say. We're still counting. That's why I called you."

"Go on." Ryder was losing patience. With Lily at home and no one to watch her, any action on his part was going to be delayed until he could drop his daughter back with his babysitter, Opal Mullins.

"There's more. Sophie insists somebody else was here, sneaking up on her. I'm not convinced. The snakes had her cornered in the yard and she was pretty paranoid about it."

Ryder clutched his phone so tightly his hand throbbed. "Is there a chance they may have been dumped there?"

"I suppose it's possible," Shane said. "Some lowlife sure has it in for our head trainer. Since the bullets missed her this morning, I did wonder if they tried to kill her with a batch of rattlers."

"Kind of hard to plan ahead for an attack like that," Ryder said. "Although I suppose they might have gathered them to release at the training center and changed their minds."

"Terrific." He snorted wryly. "Look, the worst of the danger is over and nobody was bitten. I just thought it would be good to get your input on this. You know how Harmon and Marlton can be when they're trying to avoid paperwork."

"Yeah. The sooner they retire the better," Ryder replied. "I can't believe Louise didn't call me right away. Isn't she covering the desk?"

"Not this late. So, should we hang around? Are you coming out?"

"Yes," Ryder said. "I'll have to drop Lily at the babysitter's. Give me fifteen minutes, tops."

"Copy," the rookie officer said as he prepared to end the call. "Wear your boots."

Ryder looked over at his drowsy, little blonde five-year-old and had to smile. He'd been reading her a bedtime story and she'd laid her head on the cushiony arm of the sofa when he'd stopped to answer the phone.

The sight of such a loving, beautiful child made his heart beat faster, yet constricted his gut as if he'd just taken a body blow. He'd failed to protect her mother. He was not going to fail Lily. The mere concept was abhorrent. This child was his life, his legacy, his and Melanie's, and nobody was going to harm her. He'd *die* before he'd let that happen.

He gently rubbed Lily's bare feet. "Wake up, honey. I have to go out. I'm taking you back to Miss Opal's."

"Uh-uh. It's story time. You can't go away again."

Ryder felt guilty and compensated as best he could. "How about we go out for ice cream after I get back?"

That seemed to brighten the child's mood although she was still making a face. "With sprinkles?"

"If that's what you want," Ryder promised. "Now put your shoes on while I get my boots. I need to hurry."

Lily's innocent blue eyes focused on him. "What happened, Daddy?"

"A lady found rattlesnakes in her yard."

"Are you gonna shoot them?"

Ryder couldn't tell whether the child was asking because she needed reassurance or because she felt sorry for the snakes. "I'm not sure about all of them. I imagine my officers had to shoot some."

Sadly, she said, "Oh."

"They had to protect the lady and her dog."

"Dog? She had a dog?"

"Yes."

"Like Titus?"

"Uh-huh. Kind of."

Lily began to smile. "That's different." Sitting up, she rested her bare feet on the big yellow Labrador retriever lying against the front edge of the couch and wiggled her toes into his fur. His tail thumped but he didn't rise. "I love Titus."

"Me, too," her father replied with a sigh. There was only one thing worse than having to retire a faithful canine partner and that was losing one in the line of duty. He knew it was time to give the old dog a rest, but he also knew that Titus would brood about being left behind. That was a given.

He reached down and patted the dog's broad head. "No other dog will ever work as well as you do," he said soothingly. "I don't care who says otherwise."

"Can Titus go with us?"

"Not this time, honey. You know Miss Opal's cats don't like to play with him."

The scowl returned. Nevertheless, the child had her sandals on when Ryder returned wearing his boots.

He held out his hand. "Ready?"

"No." Lily tossed her blond curls, dropped to her knees and hugged Titus's furry neck, placed a kiss on the top of his nose, then jumped to her feet. "Okay. Now I am."

The poignancy of the scene almost choked him up. So did the trusting way she grasped his fingers. Losing Melanie had nearly broken him— would have—if he hadn't had Lily. Every day that passed he loved her more. And every time he went out on a call he prayed even harder for her continued well-being.

Yes, he could have sent her away when Carrie Dunleavy's crime spree was uncovered. But that would have meant trusting his little girl to someone else's care 24/7 and he simply could not do that. No one's vigilance could be as sufficient as his because nobody could possible love Lily as much as he did. Nobody.

He'd die before he'd let anything happen to her.

Sophie wondered who in the crowd of officers combing her backyard was going give the all clear. Rookie Ellen Foxcroft was probably at the hospital visiting her comatose mother, Marian, but Shane Weston, Whitney Godwin, James Harrison and Tristan McKeller had responded. They'd done most of the actual work while Eddie Harmon and Dennis Marlton, the old-timers, had stood back and relaxed, occasionally barking an order or chuckling when one of the novices found and dealt with another snake.

"Typical," she muttered, preparing to call out to either Eddie or Dennis and insist that one of them release her to go back to the house. Before she could, they both straightened and began to feign being busy. That could mean only one thing. The chief was here.

To Sophie's amazement, the sight of Ryder's six-foot-two, athletic self brought instant relief and more than a touch of joy. He looked just as good out of uniform, in jeans and a T-shirt, as he always did with his badge on. She waved. "Over here!"

Though he paused to speak with Shane and then James, he didn't tarry long. Sweeping the beam of a flashlight ahead of him to double-check his path, he came directly to her.

"You okay?"

"I am now," she replied, having to restrain herself from leaping into his arms like a scared kid. "Thankfully my neighbors heard me shooting and reported trouble. It's been a very long evening."

"So they tell me. Why aren't you and that mutt in the house?"

"Because nobody has given us the all clear." Scowling, she eyed the part of the yard she could see from her perch. "How bad was it? I heard enough shooting and shouting to last me for the rest of my life."

A smile quirked at the corners of Ryder's mouth. "Fortunately, that will be a long time thanks to my officers." He held out his hand. "Come on. I'll get you to the house."

"I'd rather you carried Phoenix, just in case," Sophie told him. "What if they missed one?"

"Carried him?"

"Yes." She tried not to smile. "Please?"

Ryder handed her his flashlight and arched a brow. "If he bites me, we send him back where he came from tomorrow. Deal?"

That wasn't fair. She hadn't had enough time to fully assess the dog's quirks. Still, he was eventually going to have to work with the chief and had performed amiably in his initial placement so she nodded. "Okay. Go for it."

One of the important aspects of Phoenix's training regimen was going to be reinforcing his ability to adapt to many situations. This would be a good test. She snapped her fingers to get his attention, looked directly into his eyes and held up her hand, palm out. "Phoenix. Stay."

Although he flinched and tensed when Ryder slipped his arms under him and lifted, he didn't struggle. Sophie wanted to cheer.

Instead, she dropped to stand beside man and dog, pointed the light toward the house and led the way back to her porch. It was impossible to miss seeing a portion of the carnage as they passed, and its portent made her shiver.

So did the nagging feeling that someone had been watching her while she'd been trapped on the tabletop.

Ryder was spitting dog hair when he bent to lower the Aussie to the kitchen floor. To make matters worse, Phoenix turned in the blink of an eye and gave his cheek a slurp.

Sophie laughed. "Guess he won't be going back tomorrow."

"Guess not." Brushing off his civilian clothes, Ryder made a sour face. "Shedding all over me has never been a problem with Titus."

"How often do you carry him?" she asked, still chuckling. "He weighs a ton."

"I could still lift him if I needed to." Judging by the way the head trainer was eyeing his flexed biceps she wasn't going to argue. Flattered but slightly embarrassed, he changed the subject. "Let's talk about this call."

"Coffee first?" Sophie was already on her way to the counter so he nodded. "Sure."

"How about the others?"

"I told Weston to inform them they were free to return to the station. I'll send a team out at first light to clean up and make sure any possible stragglers are gone."

"Thank you."

Watching her fill two mugs with hot coffee he hoped she could carry them without spilling, since her hands were shaking so badly. "Want some help?"

"No. I've got it. Have a seat. There's sugar and creamer if you want."

"Black is fine." It didn't escape Ryder's notice that the new dog had made itself at home beneath the kitchen table and was sniffing his boots. For an animal that was supposed to be painfully shy, it seemed pretty mellow.

"Looks like you've made a friend," Sophie remarked as she joined him and slid one of the mugs across the table.

"Apparently. All I had to do was rescue him."

"And me. Thank you again."

"You're safe in here."

He saw her suppress a tremor as she replied, "For now."

He eyed the slick floor, checking shadows beneath the edge of the lower cabinets and next to the stove and refrigerator to be certain they were clear. "Do you want me to inspect the house for you?"

Sophie shook her head. "That won't be necessary. The rookies already checked. Phoenix will sense any new danger. He's the one who alerted me about the yard."

"Then why in the world did you go out?"

As he watched, she lowered her gaze and began to pick at a nonexistent spot on the tabletop. That was enough to open Ryder's eyes for the second time that day.

He cleared his throat. "I'm sorry for raising my voice, Sophie. I was just worried."

"I know." She breathed a noisy sigh. "It's been a rough evening and I put your dog in danger by not being vigilant enough. You're entitled to be upset."

Reaching for one of her trembling hands he grasped it gently. "Who said anything about the dog?"

The small kitchen seemed to shrink until all Sophie was conscious of was the strong man seated across from her. He was just being kind, she knew, yet it was awfully nice of him to hold her hand. She could certainly use the moral support.

"I've never been so scared in all my life," she admitted, blinking back unshed tears. "I took care of the big one Phoenix saw first and others near the picnic table but there were so many…"

"I know."

"And there was something else. Did your men tell you I thought there was somebody hiding and watching me while I was stranded?"

"Yes. Any idea who it might have been?"

"None. The only reason I suspected it at all was because of the way the dog bristled. I wasn't sure but he was. That's good enough for me."

"Maybe someone heard you shooting and came to see why."

Sophie scowled. "Or maybe they were already there and hoping I'd use up all my ammo and be defenseless." She trembled. "I almost did."

Feeling him squeezing her fingers a little more, she pulled her hand away. It was time to stop thinking and reacting on a personal level. She was a trained professional. She'd better start behaving like one.

Sophie sat up taller in her chair and took a sip from her mug. "All right. We can either assume it was Carrie sneaking around, unhappy that I've been talking too much to you lately, or we can look for somebody else. You and the team believe that Carrie likely didn't have an accomplice because of the journal and so-called *shrine* you found at her place, right?"

"Right."

His jaw muscles knotted visibly as he spoke, and when he clasped his hands in front of him on the table, Sophie noticed his muscles flexing. She was entitled to be upset because of her recent ordeal but Ryder had a much deeper reason. After all, Carrie's collection of memorabilia about her victims had included more than just pictures and clippings of the two blond rookies she'd killed because they'd reminded her of him. A central feature was Melanie Hayes, Ryder's late wife. Photographs and newspaper clippings on Melanie lined a wall of Carrie's bedroom. But no one figured more prominently than Ryder Hayes himself.

Empathy filled her and she placed her hand lightly atop his clenched fists. Although he flinched, he didn't withdraw until she said, "I apologize, Ryder."

"For what?"

"For being insensitive to your loss."

"Never mind that. Right now, we need to be thinking about who's trying to hurt you. Start talking."

"About what?"

"Anything. Everything. You might explain why a raised voice bothers you so much."

"I never said it did."

"You didn't have to."

"Hey, I passed my psych eval."

He didn't reply immediately and she wondered what painful questions he'd ask next. Until now she'd managed to quell her adverse reactions to triggers that mentally transported her back to her abusive childhood and she'd just as soon not awaken those feelings further.

"All right," he finally said. "Let's talk about the night your partner was shot and why you quit the force after that."

"I'd rather not."

He propped his elbows on the table and leaned forward. "I don't think you have a choice, Sophie. We have to start somewhere and that's as good a place as any. Did you receive any death threats after that incident?"

"Police officers are always being threatened," she insisted. "Almost nobody follows through."

"Maybe this guy is the exception. Criminals can be very vindictive."

The truth stuck in her throat. Was it possible Wes's brother had made good on his wild threats and come after her at this late date? Why now and not sooner? Part of her mind wanted to brush away suspicion while another part felt as if the upcoming anniversary of Wes's death might hold the answer. To voice that, however, was repugnant. The poor man and his family had suffered enough without blaming them needlessly and causing more pain.

Ryder had been studying her. "I want you to make a list of possible suspects. Don't leave anybody out no matter how innocent you think they may be. Understand?"

She nodded as she noted his darkening mood

and resigned herself to complying. "I'll do it, but I don't think you realize how difficult it will be for me."

As soon as the words left her mouth she knew she'd inadvertently been insensitive again.

Ryder's demeanor changed in a heartbeat. His eyes flashed, his jaw clamped and he stood so rapidly he almost knocked his chair over backward. Even before he said a word Sophie knew he was angry.

"Difficult?" he began. "You want to know what's difficult? Looking at my wife's picture posted with Carrie's other victims and remembering how blind I was to the evil that was right under my nose every day. *That's* difficult."

She wanted to tell him how sorry she was, how sympathetic, but she knew better than to offer platitudes when he was upset so she clasped her hands around her coffee mug and remained silent. In seconds he'd turned and stormed out the door.

Ryder was absolutely right. His loss was worse than hers in many ways. Not only had he lost his beloved Melanie and been left to raise their baby alone, he blamed himself for not considering his wife's killer could be a colleague. Carrie had presented such a mild-mannered facade they'd all been fooled.

As Sophie started to clear the table she recalled Ryder's outburst and froze in place. He'd raised his voice again. And sounded furious. So why wasn't she shaking like a leaf?

A glance toward the closed door allowed her to envision him slamming it behind him. No panic ensued. As a matter of fact, there were surprisingly warm and tender feelings flowing over and through her.

She closed her eyes and leaned on the table with both hands. Something momentous had happened tonight and it had nothing to do with snakes, at least not directly.

The emotional healing she had prayed for since she was a child had apparently begun. The scary question was, *Why?*

An even more disquieting answer came in the form of the admirable chief of police whose raised voice no longer set her nerves on edge. Why not? What had made the difference?

Phoenix came out from under the table and bumped her leg, wagging his tail and panting as he looked up expectantly. That gave Sophie her answer. She wasn't afraid of Ryder for the same reason Phoenix had accepted her.

Trust. Plain, old, heartfelt trust.

And to nurture those feelings between herself and the chief she'd eventually have to break down and name her deceased partner's disruptive brother Stan as one of her suspects.

She couldn't expect Ryder to reflect her growing sense of trust if she weren't totally honest with him.

Starting immediately.

A shiver sang up her spine and prickled at the nape of her neck. When Wes had died she'd blamed herself even more than Stan had blamed her, so his tirade at the grave site had seemed fitting.

In retrospect, it had been a lot worse than she'd realized. It wasn't merely his voice, because the threat had been whispered. It was his eyes.

There had been hate sizzling in his gaze. Hate and murderous fury. The kind that lasted. Simmered. And sometimes boiled over.

FOUR

As soon as Ryder left Sophie he headed straight for Mrs. Mullins's home to pick up Lily. When he arrived at the small, Spanish-style house, he lingered outside in his cruiser long enough to regain the strong self-control on which he prided himself. A man in command could not afford to show anger or weakness or any other emotion that would be detrimental to his position. More importantly, he didn't want to upset his little Lily.

He found her in the living room, playing with Opal's cats and telling them all about her wonderful dog. Maybe it was time to retire Titus. Yes, he got very excited when Ryder strapped on his official K-9 harness or vest but Sophie was right. He also tired easily.

Opal joined him in the archway to the living room when he paused to listen to the involved tale Lily was telling.

"She's been like this ever since you dropped her off," the middle-aged woman said. "What in the world did you tell her? She keeps warning my cats to look out for bad snakes."

"We had a call tonight, over at the head trainer's place. She was shooting snakes."

"The slithery kind or the two-legged kind?"

"Slithery. She just about emptied her gun until she remembered about the human kind of snake and saved a shot or two. Maybe now she'll carry an extra clip."

Opal smiled, brown eyes twinkling, and patted the waist of her jeans. "I keep mine on an empty chamber, for safety. Staying alert is important for old ladies who live alone, particularly when there's so much trouble in town. Besides, I have your girl to think of."

"Why do you think I trust you with Lily?" Ryder asked, returning her smile. "Anybody who was an MP is bound to be a good, safe guard."

"That was a long time ago."

"You never forget," he countered. "It's like riding a bicycle. The programming sticks in your mind."

"And muscle memory." Opal's grin spread. "Wanna see me fieldstrip a .45 auto blindfolded?"

"Maybe later." Ryder eyed his child. "I promised the princess some ice cream."

"You spoil her."

"And love every minute of it," he said.

That made Opal chuckle. "Wait until she's a teenager, and then tell me you feel the same way."

He sobered. "I'm not in any hurry."

Her touch on his arm was gentle, motherly. "You should think about a mama for her, you know. Every girl needs a mother, particularly as she gets older."

Ryder chose to turn the serious moment into a joke and arched an eyebrow. "Are you applying for the job?"

"Hah! I sure would if I was about thirty years younger. Of course, if you like your ladies real mature..." Opal patted her short cropped hair with one hand and rested the other on her hip.

"I'll keep you in mind," Ryder promised. "I know you can cook."

"Yup. And I shoot straight, too."

"Yeah." His eyes were on Lily. "I just wish this was a peaceful little town again. Even after losing Melanie it seemed relatively safe here. Everybody thought her murder was an isolated incident for a long time."

Opal sighed. "I know what you mean. How were we to know those other two fellas were victims, too? How'd that Carrie person choose 'em in the first place?"

"Because they reminded her of me," he said quietly. "I told you she killed Melanie out of jealousy. After that, she apparently fixated on a rookie officer who had light-colored hair like mine. When Mike Riverton didn't ask her for a date to the Police Dance two years ago she made his death look like an accident by pushing him down stairs. The following year, Brian Miller ignored her too and ended up dying in a fire when his house went up in flames."

"You never told me all that before."

Ryder nodded. "We held back details about the case and Carrie's motive to keep from causing a panic. Besides, Veronica Earnshaw didn't fit the victim profile."

Staring at him earnestly, the older woman said, "No, but Carrie might have thought you were interested in her."

"We can't rule it out," Ryder told her. "That's a big reason why I don't dare show favoritism to *any* woman. Not until Carrie's caught and jailed."

"Meaning, no dating." Opal turned to gaze fondly at Lily. "That's too bad."

"It's more than just dating. It's what goes on at work, too. If Carrie even imagines I'm spending too much time with another woman, that woman will be in danger." *Like Sophie has been.*

He shivered, then pulled himself together and banished destructive thoughts as he called out to his daughter. "Time to go, Lily. If we don't get there before the Cactus Café closes, we'll have to buy our ice cream at the mini mart."

She proceeded to tell each cat goodbye before getting to her feet. "They want to go, too, Daddy."

"Miss Opal doesn't want them outside," he countered.

"'Cause of the snakes, huh?"

"Right. And traffic and coyotes and all kinds of dangers. They were raised inside. This is what they know."

"But you could protect them, Daddy. You can do anything," Lily said, gazing up at him in adoration.

"I wish I could." Ryder was thinking back to the night he'd been too caught up in his job to pick up his wife from town. That was the night Melanie had been ambushed.

In Ryder's mind, no matter who had actually shot and killed her, part of the blame belonged to him. He'd be atoning for the rest of his life.

Grasping Lily's hand and holding tight he led her to the door, then paused to peer out into the yard. Nobody, Carrie Dunleavy included, was ever going to take someone he loved from him again. Not while he still had breath in his body.

And after that? He set his jaw. He knew he should trust God in all things, even the life of his darling Lily, but he kept remembering Melanie. They had believed together that the Lord had blessed their marriage, so why had He allowed her to be taken?

An overwhelming sense of doom enveloped him. He scooped his daughter into his arms, held her tight and jogged to the patrol car. This must be the way Sophie had felt when she'd imagined a menace besides the snakes, he concluded. Instinct for self-preservation had kicked in and she'd reacted to it on a basic level.

One thing was clear. Some gut feelings were God-given and had better be heeded. To ignore them was not only foolish, it was akin to laughing in the face of his heavenly Father.

"Forgive me, Lord," Ryder whispered as he fastened Lily in the backseat. A scripture verse popped into his head. "Lord, I believe. Help Thou my unbelief."

No lightning bolts shot down from heaven. No angels sang. But Ryder was calmer, stronger, more self-assured as he circled to the driver's side of the car. The Desert Valley police were going to catch whoever had been threatening Sophie, whether it turned out to be Carrie or not. As chief, he would see to it.

Only one thing took priority. The innocent little girl in the backseat. She always would.

Nervous despite her dog and reloaded pistol, Sophie had trouble sleeping. It didn't help that Phoenix hogged the bed. She shoved him over and threw back the covers as soon as the sun began to peek over the top of the red rock horizon. Morning was usually one of her favorite times in the desert, with fresh, cooler air and pristine silence.

Today, however, she had enthusiastic company. Phoenix spun in circles at her feet and raced from the room as soon as her bare feet touched the floor. "Okay, okay. I'm coming."

Not knowing how well he was trained, she figured it would be smart to slip some clothes on and let him out quickly. Boots didn't exactly go with cargo shorts but she wasn't letting her dog set foot in the backyard until she was sure there were no live snakes left.

She snapped a leash on his collar, tucked her gun into one of the pockets on the shorts and opened the back door. Except for remnants of last night's carnage, the place looked deserted. Sophie hesitated. There was no guarantee that her front yard was clear, either, but at least it wasn't messy, so she opted to reverse direction and lead Phoenix out that way instead of turning him loose inside the fenced area.

While he sniffed and wandered, unconcerned and therefore safe, Sophie checked the ground around the sides of her house. During her nocturnal unrest she'd reasoned that she'd been imagining hidden menaces so it was a shock to come upon wadded-up gum wrappers in the very place where she'd thought she'd sensed danger lurking.

"Oh, my..."

Her reaction was strong enough to cause the dog to take up a defensive position with his side pressed to her leg and hackles raised.

She laid a comforting hand on his head. "Good

boy. I think we're all right now but I'm going to call this in."

Backing off, she led Phoenix away in order to keep from contaminating possible clues. As soon as she started to dial 911 she thought better of it. The last thing she needed was to cause a full-blown police response when the clues might mean nothing, and she sure didn't want to phone James Harrison and ask for his bloodhound when he was romantically involved with *Canyon County Gazette* reporter Madison Coles who would be likely to want to put her in the news. Sophie then thought about summoning Whitney but she was a single mother with a baby to take care of and it was barely dawn.

"Face it," Sophie muttered, disgusted with herself. "You aren't fooling anybody. You want to call Ryder."

He also had a child, but Lily was old enough to bring along if he chose. Besides, it would be advantageous to introduce Phoenix to Lily on neutral ground.

"Right. I need to be sure the dog likes kids," Sophie told herself, immediately recognizing the excuse for what it was. Lame. However, that was not enough to keep her from calling him at home.

Instead of making small talk, Sophie began with, "I found some clues—chewing gum papers and foil—next to my house. I'm pretty sure they weren't there before."

"I take it this is Sophie."

"Of course it is. I told you I was being watched. Suppose there's DNA on the gum wrappers? I didn't stop to see if there was any old gum lying around. I didn't touch a thing and I kept the dog back, too."

"Good for you."

"Look, do you want me to call somebody else? I don't particularly want a bunch of red lights and sirens charging over here again, not after the uproar last night. Which reminds me. Didn't you say you'd come check the yard this morning? How is that any different than coming by now?"

"Well, for one thing Lily wouldn't be with me later."

Sophie suddenly saw his concerns. "You're afraid to bring her here?"

He huffed. "I'm afraid to let her out of my sight, period."

"I understand. Now that I think about it, I know I've noticed that brand of gum at either the police station or training center. I just can't place exactly where. I could pick up the evidence and keep it clean but it wouldn't be admissible in court since I'm no longer an officer of the law."

Ryder yawned. "What are you asking me to do?"

"Come and get it."

"I have minions for that."

Sophie could tell he was chuckling and was

not amused. "I was trying to keep from making a big fuss about it and getting everybody all riled up. You want to keep the good citizens of Desert Valley calm, don't you?"

"Yes." Another yawn. "Okay. Leave your evidence alone and keep the dog from getting into it. I'll get dressed and be there as soon as I can."

"Why don't you come for coffee? If you change your mind and bring Lily I can fix pancakes for us all."

"Not a good idea," Ryder countered. "I don't think it's wise for me to be seen spending any private time with you."

Sophie wanted to ask him if he was afraid of Carrie or of himself. She didn't. Instead, she said, "Consider it a part of Phoenix's training. I'd like to make sure he's good with children."

"Then meet us at the office some afternoon."

"You're right. Sorry. I'll stay here and wait. Will you come by as soon as you drop her off?"

When Ryder said, "Yes," Sophie felt such relief she almost sighed aloud.

She wasn't afraid of facing enemies she could see. It was the hidden ones that set her nerves on edge. The ones like the gunman who had killed her partner while she was tracking another criminal.

Or the ones who patiently lurked in the shadows and chewed gum while they watched her try to keep from being poisoned by snake venom.

No matter what anybody said, she still suspected that those snakes had been dumped over her back fence to do what vipers did best. To kill.

Ryder had donned his full uniform so he could go on to work once he was finished gathering evidence at Sophie's. Her front door swung open before he reached the porch.

"Thanks for coming."

He touched the brim of his cap. "Where's the evidence?"

"Over there." She gestured. "I'll come with you."

Waiting at the corner of the house until she joined him, he scowled. "Where?"

"Right…" Her jaw dropped. "It was right *there*."

It went against his high opinion of her to doubt but he certainly had questions. "Could you be mistaken?"

"No, I saw foil and paper gum wrappers. Most of them were crumpled up so they wouldn't be likely to blow away. Besides, there's no breeze stirring this morning."

Ryder arched an eyebrow. "That was my conclusion. So, what do you think happened to them?"

"How should I know?" Her voice was raised, her eyes wide. "They have to be here somewhere."

"All right. We'll circle the house first, then bring in a dog."

Clearly, Sophie believed she'd seen clues, which

was a point in her favor. Being unable to lead him to the scene was not.

"It was near this back corner," she insisted. "The same area that had me spooked last night. Remember what I told you about saving ammo just in case? Well, this was where Phoenix was looking when I started to feel as if we were being watched."

"So you assumed you'd see clues this morning?"

"No. I wasn't even thinking of that when I stumbled on the gum wrappers."

"Maybe. Maybe not."

Whirling, she fisted her hands on her hips. If Ryder hadn't been so disgusted to have been talked into participating in a wild-goose chase, he might have smiled at her uncompromising demeanor.

"I did not imagine a thing, Chief," she said with conviction. "There were clues on the ground. Look. See the footprints?"

"Most every cop in Desert Valley was walking out here last night," Ryder reminded her. "Any of them could have been chewing gum."

"Okay, okay. Suppose you radio the station and ask if they were before you assume I'm lying."

"I never said you were lying. I do wonder if your imagination isn't working overtime, though. You were pretty freaked out last night."

"Do you blame me?"

"Nope. It did surprise me that you assumed the snakes were part of a planned attack. The Arizona desert is their natural habitat. You must know they den up for winter."

"It's August and hotter than ever," Sophie countered. "I know how snakes behave. If there was a den in my backyard I think I'd have discovered it by now. I've lived here for two summers."

"Something around you may have changed. They could have lost their regular underground access to tunnels and been forced to seek another way in."

"I'd think you'd be the first to suspect an attack, especially after I was shot at in the depot."

As she spoke, Ryder was slowly making his way around her house. Roadrunners and flocks of smaller birds were busy cleaning up the mess near the back fence, making his job easier in one way.

He straightened when they returned to their starting point. "I suppose jays or some other species might have been attracted to the shiny wrappers and carried them off."

"Birds? You're blaming birds?"

Ryder let her barely controlled anger roll off him. Even if Phoenix didn't strike a trail, Titus would let them know if there had been a prowler. "Go get the new dog and let's see what he does."

"Not on your life."

"I beg your pardon?"

"You should," Sophie told him. "If you gave my

opinion a shred of credit you wouldn't tell me to get a dog we know so little about. You'd bring in Titus and do the search properly."

When she was right, she was right. Ryder nodded. "My apologies. I'll go get Titus out of the car."

"I should hope so."

He could tell that Sophie was still miffed. Unfortunately, she'd been right when she'd guessed that he wasn't treating her so-called report of clues seriously. Either she'd imagined seeing signs of a lurker or she'd invented one. There was no way things like that just disappeared on a totally windless morning. At least not so completely. When he'd mentioned the birds in the area he'd been giving her a chance to alibi away her error in judgment. Now she was going to be stuck with it.

Opening the rear door of his SUV he fitted the working dog with a special K-9 vest, snapped a long lead on his collar and signaled him to get out.

Titus's tail wagged as eagerly as ever but his steps were slightly halting until he got warmed up. Knowing that the head trainer was observing them made Ryder extra cautious. Since they had nothing with which to offer a scent to the dog, he began to lead him in a circuitous path before rejoining Sophie.

She didn't greet the happy dog as she would have under casual circumstances. Instead, she motioned to the ground where she'd noticed the bits of trash and said, "Seek."

Ryder didn't expect any reaction, let alone a strong one. The old dog snuffled the ground, disturbing dried grass and leaves, then kept his nose to the ground, wheeled and headed directly for the street.

Playing out the light lead, Ryder followed. Titus had not only struck a trail, he was acting as if the scent was fresh!

If he hadn't been so biased in the first place, Ryder would have easily concluded that someone had returned recently and picked up the gum wrappers that Sophie had spotted. Now he was forced to reconsider.

Titus led him to the curb, then up the street several houses before he lost the trail.

Disgusted with himself and slightly contrite, Ryder turned to Sophie. "I owe you an apology. Somebody was in your yard, probably this morning, and they got into a car right here. We'll need to check with the nearest residents to see if they noticed."

"We can hope," she said.

Frowning, he took her by the elbow and ushered her back to her house as quickly as possible.

"What's the hurry? The gum chewer is gone."

"Now, maybe," Ryder said gruffly. "But stop and think. The only way anyone would have known you'd stumbled on those wrappers was by watching you do it."

To his relief, Sophie took him seriously. "And coming to clean them up before you arrived."

"That would be my conclusion, yes."

She paled and rested a hand on his forearm before she said, "I'm so glad you didn't bring Lily."

Heart racing, he scanned the surrounding properties for any sign of danger. Not seeing anything out of the ordinary didn't mean there wasn't a lingering threat.

One he might have walked his little girl right into if he hadn't been so worried about letting Carrie see him visiting another woman.

Now he was left wondering if she actually had.

FIVE

After their fruitless time outside, Sophie had hoped Ryder would stay for coffee. He begged off.

She vented by talking to the dog. "It's just you and me, boy. We can have scrambled eggs if you want. What do you say? A little people food won't hurt you."

Phoenix responded to her lilting tone with enthusiasm that left no doubt he'd be thrilled no matter what she fed him. Gazing up at her adoringly, he wagged his stub of a tail so rapidly his whole rear half did a frenetic hula.

"You're going to make it, aren't you, boy? Yes, you are. And as soon as we've eaten you can have the first lesson in your refresher course."

Taking Phoenix to the training center was a given. Keeping him with her at home was optional. It was hard for Sophie to admit she wished she could keep him indefinitely. He was not only company, he was a kindred spirit.

"Just like Ryder," she murmured. "Only I understand dogs a lot better than I do people. Guess I always have."

And that's where my God-given gifts lie, she added silently. It was a lot easier to picture herself in the midst of a litter of wiggly puppies than working at a preschool surrounded by sticky-fingered toddlers. The silly impression made her chuckle.

Being around Phoenix had lifted her spirits more than she'd expected. His joie de vivre was infectious. It was going to be a real pleasure to rescue him from his doldrums and give him a new purpose in life.

That goal was still on her mind an hour later when she pulled into the training center lot and parked. There were fenced areas for off-lead work, obstacle courses, search areas where officers could hide drugs for the dogs to find, and even a yard for pups that she was evaluating and training.

Then there was the Desert Valley Canine Assistance Dog Center. When Ellen Foxcroft had suggested starting that program she'd met with a lot of resistance, including Sophie's, but everybody was now convinced the project was worthwhile. It took a special mentality for a dog to provide stable, reliable assistance to the disabled without getting excited and endangering them. Police dogs were very different from companion animals.

Sophie smiled down at Phoenix as she led him toward her K-9 facility. He had all the intelligence and instinct needed to partner with a police officer. He'd succeeded once. He'd do it again—if she had anything to say about it.

Entering the building she led the Australian shepherd on a meet and greet, beginning with Louise Donaldson's desk. The dark-haired, sixty-ish widow smiled slightly. "So, this is the infamous Phoenix. Do you expect him to rise from the ashes like his mythical namesake?"

"I certainly hope so," Sophie replied.

"He seems to be pretty calm this morning."

"We're making progress."

As she turned to proceed, Gina Perry, her junior trainer, was entering with Shane Weston and his German shepherd, Bella. He kept his suspect apprehension dog on a short leash. Her fawn-and-black coat bristled and her body language predicted aggression.

Sophie acknowledged his sensible actions. "Thanks, Shane. I don't want Phoenix in a dogfight. Bella could have him for breakfast and never even breathe hard."

"He is kinda cute," Shane said. "What's his specialty?"

Gina answered for her boss. "Search and rescue. He used to be really good at it. We're hoping we can rehab him."

"If anybody can, you two can," Shane said. Considering the fact he had eyes only for Gina,

Sophie was surprised he'd included them both in his praise.

Whitney Godwin breezed in, her light blond hair pulled into a tight knot, blue eyes wide. "Sorry I'm late. Shelby was fussy this morning. I think she's teething."

"I won't tell," Sophie said, picturing Whitney's adorable baby daughter. "Meet Phoenix."

"Oooh, can I pet him?"

"In this case, yes. I'm trying to accustom him to crowds and help him relax. He really is a sweetheart."

From behind her, Sophie heard a familiar voice ask, "Who's a sweetheart?" Her first thought was of Ryder but the speaker was rookie James Harrison.

"This Aussie," Sophie countered. "And your bloodhound. Hawk is more laid-back, though. Phoenix was pretty hyper this morning."

"Maybe he knows he has a new lease on life. Which reminds me," James drawled, "Madison would like to interview you about the depot shooting."

"It's all in the official reports. Nothing more to tell." Turning away, Sophie hoped neither he nor his reporter girlfriend would tie the snake incident and the shooting together. At least not yet.

"So, where's Tristan this morning?" Sophie asked.

"Investigating a possible arson in a seasonal

cabin," Louise explained. "Probably vandalism. City kids think it's fun to come out here and do things they'd never try at home, as if we're too rural to figure things out."

Sophie nodded and looked over the room with its scattered desks, some of which had to be shared due to space and funding. "We do have an advantage right now," she said. "Once Carrie's in custody, I wonder if Marian Foxcroft's money will stop coming in to fund us." Just as she finished speaking she noticed Ellen Foxcroft in the background and apologized. "Oops. Sorry, Ellen. I didn't mean to sound disrespectful. How is your mom? Any better?"

Ellen smiled wistfully. "The specialists keep saying she'll come out of the coma soon. She's been showing hopeful signs."

"Good. I'm so glad. How's your special guy, Lee Earnshaw?"

"Going back to school to become a veterinarian," Ellen said, beginning to beam with pride.

"That's wonderful. He was so good with dogs when we met in the Prison Pups program."

"Good can come out of anything, right? Even Lee being framed for something he didn't do. I think Veronica would finally be proud of her brother."

The mention of her murdered predecessor, Veronica Earnshaw, dampened Sophie's mood. Phoenix sensed the change immediately and became more subdued.

"Well, I guess we'd all better get back to work before the chief catches us gabbing," Sophie said, trying to appear lighthearted. She looked around for one more rookie. "Where's Tristan going after he finishes investigating the fire?"

"Probably to make sure his teenage sister stays out of trouble," someone joked.

Sophie felt a smile coming on and encouraged it. "I never got into trouble when I was a kid."

She hadn't noticed Ryder entering the office so when he said, "What did you do, save it all for now?" she whirled. Her cheeks warmed. She barely managed, "Morning, Chief."

He nodded and proceeded to his office. Sophie figured this was a good time to make her exit, so she headed for the training center, a quarter of a mile up the street from the police station.

The aroma of freshly brewed coffee told her that Gina had stopped there before joining Shane at the DVPD. The gentle, auburn-haired, junior trainer was a perfect foil for Sophie's personality. They were a much better fit than either of them had been with Veronica. Nevertheless, the deceased woman had been great with dogs. It was her approach to humans that had been hard to take.

Sophie took her time, checked phone messages, followed up on some donations of young dogs she was considering and sipped a cup of hot coffee. All the while, Phoenix lay at her feet, tucked into the knee space beneath her desk.

The officers and rookies had unanimously decided to turn the upstairs apartment into a break area and storage after Veronica's murder. Sophie certainly didn't want to live there when she was well settled in the house on Second Street. Besides, they needed the extra room for equipment. One thing on her to-do list this morning was fitting Phoenix with a work vest and harness to see if they made any difference in his behavior.

As soon as she completed her paperwork she rinsed her cup, put it away with the others and led the dog upstairs. Even with the AC running, the rooms were stuffy. She'd have opened a window for ventilation if she'd arrived earlier. By now, it was too hot. Outside temps climbed fast in summer and fall, even though desert nights tended to be cool.

Boxes of collars, harnesses and vests were stashed in the main closet. It didn't take Sophie's trained eye long to choose the correct size working vest and fit it to the Australian shepherd. He didn't act pleased.

"Hey, buddy, you have to wear your badge and patches or you'll look just like every other cute pet out there," Sophie lectured, keeping her tone mellow. She ruffled his ears and patted his head. "Come on. Time to practice."

Phoenix threw himself to the floor and rolled onto his back.

Not good. She straightened and exerted control by voice, stature and actions. "Phoenix, heel."

Although he did stand, his head was hanging. If he'd had a tail he'd have tucked it between his legs.

Sophie began to walk away as if she fully expected him to behave. He did. Up to a point. By the time they reached the ground floor Phoenix had almost caught up to her.

Pausing in front of the door to the training yard, she waited for him to sit at her side. When he eased his rear down as if being asked to sit on cactus needles, she almost laughed. Poor guy. He wanted to be good but instinctive fear kept him from it, and until he was over that, there was no use setting up a search and rescue scenario.

The dog lover in her wanted to hug away his fears but she knew that wouldn't help. If she demonstrated concern she'd only reinforce his reluctance to perform.

"Heel," she said firmly, stepping out into the training yard.

Head drooping, he nevertheless obeyed. That was a good sign. It meant he was willing to follow her into unfamiliar territory. Score one point for the trainer.

Sophie marched around the obstacles in the large yard, keeping Phoenix at her side. Few commands were necessary. Even better, he was no longer acting as if he was being led to his own execution. He wasn't exactly jubilant but at least he looked reasonably self-assured.

She took out a canvas training toy and waved it at him. His eyes brightened. Paws danced. Stubby tail wagged.

"Aha. You do remember, don't you, boy."

She unclipped the leash, told him to sit, then gave him the toy as a reward. The change was complete. Phoenix was happy again. Deliriously so. He did want to work. And he did want his reward for doing so.

Sophie was so engrossed in watching the new dog play, she failed to pay attention to her surroundings.

Phoenix suddenly dropped his toy at her feet and growled. It took Sophie several seconds to figure out he was looking through the chain-link fence at a dark-colored car slowly passing in the street. There was no reason for him to be concerned so she reprimanded him. "No."

The dog was not deterred. His snug vest kept his hackles from rising visibly but there was no doubt he was being protective.

She shaded her eyes with one hand. The car came to a full stop. The driver's window rolled down. Something was sticking out the opening. It almost looked like...

"Gun!" Sophie shouted, reverting to her police

training. She dived for cover behind a wooden training structure that looked like a tiny house.

The sharp crack of a bullet being fired split the morning air.

Gina appeared in the office doorway. "What's going on?"

"Get back!" Sophie shouted, waving her arms. "Call 911. Somebody's shooting at me!"

Gina screamed and disappeared.

Sophie stayed behind the small structure. *Phoenix! Where was Phoenix?* Could the attacker have been aiming at him? Surely not. The dog hadn't done anything wrong.

No, but police dogs were occasionally killed by criminals, Sophie reminded herself. Reading about such senseless loss always made her sad—and angry. Very angry.

She drew her pistol and rose up high enough to see the street. The car was still there. The dog was flat on the ground about ten feet from her.

"Phoenix! Come."

He raised his head and began to crawl toward her while she kept her aim directed at the black vehicle. If anybody tried to fire again she intended to stop them.

The dog was at her side in seconds, panting and trembling. Sophie pulled him close and checked for injuries as armed officers raced to surround the strange car and block its path.

There was a little blood on the dog's front paw.

Sophie was about to try to carry him to the vet's office next door when she realized the blood she saw was dripping from her own forehead!

Only then did she notice a slight stinging sensation. She poked the spot with her index finger. It came away red.

Ryder and his men boxed in the black vehicle with their own cars, approached with guns drawn, and ordered the occupants to raise their hands and get out slowly. The side windows had been darkened so much it was impossible to see the interior.

Several of the K-9s were more interested in the ground around the car than the car itself. Once Shane had worked his way to the front and peered through the windshield, he signaled for Marlton and Whitney Godwin to breach the doors. The car was empty. The shooter or shooters had gotten away.

If Ryder hadn't left Titus behind in the office he would have put him on the trail immediately. Instead, he pointed to Ellen Foxcroft and her golden retriever, Carly. "Start your dog tracking. Weston, you back her up with Bella. If the scent splits, you two do the same. I want this guy."

Shane touched two fingers to his brow. "Yes, sir. We're looking for a man?"

"I wish I knew. It might be Carrie Dunleavy, and it might not. I have Sophie making me a list of possible assailants. I'll start Louise working on it as soon as I get the names."

As some of his officers dispersed, he assigned Harrison to work up the evidence, not that he expected this perp to have left behind any clues. He'd already noted no shell casings on the floor of the vehicle or outside on the road. That much caution probably meant there would be no fingerprints, either.

There were times, like now, when he almost wished he could blame Carrie for everything. At least that way they'd be able to focus entirely on capturing her. One of his worst fears was that she might have joined forces with some other criminal, maybe one she'd met while working for the DVPD. The concept made him shiver despite the blinding sun.

Ryder was headed back to his patrol car when his cell phone rang. It was Tanya Fowler's number. "Hayes here."

"Hey, chief," the veterinarian said. "I've got a little problem. I may need your help."

"I was told there were no injuries. Was one of the dogs hurt?"

"Nope," the vet said.

His pulse had just begun to slow when she added, "This patient is much harder to handle. I can't put her in a cage and a muzzle won't fit."

Ryder was in no mood for jokes. "What are you talking about?"

She lowered her voice until she was rasping into the phone. "There's a stubborn trainer sitting on my exam table right now and insisting I bandage a scalp wound. I don't want to get in trouble with Doc Evans or the clinic. Do you think you could convince her to go to the ER?"

"Sophie?" It had to be. His heart returned to double time. "What happened to her?"

"She's not hurt badly. I just think she should have Evans check her over, for her sake as much as mine."

"I'll be right there." Ryder threw himself behind the wheel of his car. *Sophie again.* She drew trouble the way flowers drew honeybees. So what did that make him?

"Crazy," he murmured to himself. If he wasn't already, he would be soon, thanks to the trainer facing one disaster after another.

He made a face, said, "I can hardly wait for the next incident," before he realized that the next attack might do her much more serious harm. Or worse.

SIX

"I'm fine, I tell you. Just clean it up and slap a butterfly bandage on it," Sophie insisted.

Tanya shook her head and backed away, hands raised as if she were being robbed. "No way. I could get in legal trouble."

"I won't tell."

"It's still wrong. If this is a gunshot. I'm not touching it."

Sophie had been pressing a paper towel to her forehead, just below the hairline. She flashed a contrite look. "It's not. I'm sure I just whacked my head on the corner of one of the training structures when I dived for cover. There's no sense making a big deal out of it and going to the ER."

She swiveled at the sound of running boots in the hallway. The sight of Ryder was welcome despite the thunder in his expression when he burst through the door.

It was Sophie's turn to hold up her hands to reassure him but she didn't want to move the paper towel so she used only one hand, raising it like a traffic cop on a busy corner. "I'm okay. Relax. It really isn't serious."

She thought for a moment he might sag against the doorjamb but he recovered quickly.

"What happened? I was told nobody was hit."

She winced. "I was just telling Tanya. I think I bumped my head when I took cover. I wasn't shot."

"How do you know? Have you been shot before?"

"No, but..."

He grabbed latex gloves from an open box on the counter and pulled them on before approaching Sophie. She wanted to fend him off, to tell him she'd take care of herself, but given his concern and commanding nature she decided to hold back.

His touch was gentle as he moved her hand away and disposed of the paper towel. "The bleeding has almost stopped. How long since you had a tetanus shot?"

"I hate shots."

"So do the dogs, but you make sure they're immunized."

She shrugged. He had a point. "Okay. I can call the clinic and have them check my records."

Ryder was stripping off the gloves. "Where's Phoenix?"

"Gina has him. Why?"

"Because you and I are going to see David

Evans in person. He can check your medical records then."

"And assure you I wasn't shot. He was an army medic in Afghanistan. He'll know on sight."

Ryder took Sophie's arm and helped her off the steel table. "Evans is a good man," Sophie continued. "Whitney's blessed to have him in her life. He'll be a good father for her baby. It's nice for kids to have two..."

She stopped herself but not in time. Ryder's closed expression proved he knew she'd been going to refer to two parents, something his Lily didn't have. Sophie could have slapped herself for being so thoughtless.

In an effort the soften the blow she added, "I had both parents and I'd have been better off with neither. They fought all the time. I felt as if I was raised in a war zone."

They were nearly out the front door. "Is that why you chose law enforcement?" Ryder asked.

Surely he already knew that, she reasoned, meaning he was probably making conversation in hopes of distracting her from where they were going. Nevertheless, she played along. "Yes. And dog training. My best friends were animals. They still are."

His grip on her arm tightened almost imperceptibly, but it did change. She'd have loved hearing why, particularly if he was feeling sorry for her. That sentiment was not permitted. She'd wasted too much time brooding as a teen to allow anybody to drag her back down into despair. Her life was fine. She was fine. And no good-looking, bossy cop, chief or not, was going to get away with pitying her. No sir.

Straightening, she reclaimed her arm and quickly climbed into his cruiser. When he slid behind the wheel she was ready for him.

"If you won't do this my way, at least take me by my house so I can get a change of clothes."

"You keep spare clothes in your locker."

"I used them and forgot to bring more."

Although he arched an eyebrow he capitulated. "All right. But the clinic first."

"You're really stubborn, you know that?"

Ryder stared. "I'm stubborn? Compared to you I'm a pushover. Which reminds me. Do you have that suspect list ready for me? I want Louise to get on it ASAP."

"Well…"

"Have you even started it?"

"In my head," Sophie said.

He pulled a clipboard from beside his seat and handed it to her. "Write."

"Now?"

"Yes, now. Before your thoughts get any more scrambled than they already are."

Sophie huffed. "My thoughts are not scrambled. I just have a lot to think about and my brain is always busy."

"If you expect me to accept that as the reason why you didn't notice you were under fire, forget it." He rolled his eyes. "Considering all that's happened to you in the past few days you should be on high alert at all times."

"I am. I was." She gestured at her clothing. "As hot as it is, I still wore my bulletproof vest this morning."

"And now?"

"It's back at Tanya's office because I didn't want to drip on it. I'll get it later."

Sophie noticed his white-knuckle grip on the steering wheel right before he said, "I hope nobody takes another shot at you before you do."

Evans had confirmed Sophie was not shot, given her a tetanus booster and done exactly what she'd asked of the vet. That didn't particularly please Ryder. The woman was already so self-confident she was almost unbearable. Adding support from other professionals was likely to make her worse. If that was possible.

"I still want to go to my house," she insisted after they were back in the car.

Ryder wasn't surprised. "I figured you would."

"Smart man."

"No," he said flatly. "If I were smart I'd have put you on paid leave as soon as you were shot at the first time."

"I wouldn't have left town."

"Yeah, I figured that, too." He made a sour face at her. "This way, at least I know where you are and there are plenty of cops nearby. If you aren't worried for yourself, you should at least be concerned about the dogs you train."

"I am. But whoever is upset with me doesn't seem to be targeting animals," she argued. "That's a plus."

"A plus would be finding a viable suspect on the list you finally made. I've decided to have you work with Louise to track those people down. The sooner we have addresses for each of them, the sooner we can start crossing off names."

"More paperwork?" Sophie sighed. "I have Phoenix to work with and a couple of younger dogs to assess for Ellen's assistant dog program. I don't have time to waste shuffling papers."

"Do you have time to waste in the hospital?" Ryder considered adding the morgue and thought better of it. Sophie was intelligent. She'd make the correlation without him spelling it out.

"I can't run forever."

"No, but you can keep your head down." He let himself smile at her look of consternation. "Pun intended, by the way."

"Ha-ha." She lightly touched the bandage. "I did this ducking. If I'd stood still I wouldn't have a scratch."

"Providing the shooter didn't fire again." He

scowled at her. "Do you argue with everybody or is it just me?"

"I'm not arguing."

"You could have fooled me." Ryder wheeled into her driveway and shut off the motor. Instead of allowing Sophie to enter the house alone, he followed. Closely.

"I don't need help."

"I'm not here to help you. I'm here for protection."

Although she rolled her eyes, she didn't refuse his company. That was a plus. So was her cooperation when he insisted on searching the house before parking himself in the living room to wait for her to freshen up.

From there he could hear her banging doors and mumbling to herself. It was when she grew quiet that he tensed. "Are you all right?"

"Yes."

The answer was satisfactory but her tone was not. As he started down the hall he heard water running. "Are you dressed?"

"Yes. I'll be out in a minute."

The door to the bathroom stood ajar. Sophie was leaning sideways over the sink and trying to rinse her blond hair without wetting the injury. There were tears in her eyes.

He sighed. "Here. Let me do that. You're making a mess."

"I can wash my own hair."

"I'm sure you can. But you can't see what you're doing without looking in the mirror and if you do that, the soapy water is going to run right into that cut."

She winced. "I know. I already tried."

This is a mistake, Ryder's conscience insisted. Yet he reached for her. Touched her silky hair. Cupped his hand beneath the faucet and slowly rinsed her hair.

She'd closed her eyes and was breathing deeply, as if his ministrations had calmed her. Time stopped. Ryder didn't want it to ever start again. He watched the water stream through her hair and over the fingers of his other hand. He had not been this close to a woman since Melanie and it didn't matter how innocent his actions had been in the beginning, they were now eliciting feelings that were far too tender, too extraordinary.

Ryder snapped himself out of the emotional trap and reached for a towel. He started to press it to her scalp, then changed his mind and stepped back.

"There. You're presentable. Just dry it a little and I'll take you to work."

When Sophie opened her eyes and looked at him she seemed every bit as off-kilter as he felt. Her cheeks were rosy, her hazel eyes glowing, glittering.

Ryder touched her shoulder when she wavered. "You okay?"

"A little dizzy," she said, then smiled. "From hanging over the sink, not from banging my head."

"If you say so." Backing away as he spoke, he kept one hand reaching toward her in case she faltered again. "I'll go check the yard and street. Come out when you're ready."

"Wait." She straightened. Her smile lessened into an expression that was very different from what he was used to from her. "I want to thank you. For everything."

For making a fool of myself just now? Ryder asked himself before rejecting the idea. Only he knew how special it had felt to help her, to touch her hair, to be that close without letting his emotions show.

"Doing my job," he alibied, turning away. "I'll be outside."

By the time he reached her front door he was back in cop mode. He'd better be, he cautioned himself. Somebody was out to get his head trainer and until they were able to whittle down the list she'd given them, there was no telling who or what awaited Sophie Williams.

Easing the door open, Ryder kept one hand on his holster. The sleepy little desert town he'd been charged with protecting had turned into a jungle, filled with predators ready to attack.

As long as he never let down his guard everything should be all right. But he couldn't be everywhere. Neither could his officers, even with the rookies working as temps and his veterans putting off planned retirements.

All any of them could do was try. And pray. And hope that the shooter, whoever he or she was, continued to miss. The way Ryder saw it, it was only a matter of time before more fatalities occurred.

Visualizing the whiteboard in his office he pictured Sophie among the victims.

What shocked and surprised him the most was that his vivid imagination had inserted her photo in place of Melanie's.

Sophie studied herself in the bathroom mirror. She didn't see the difference she was feeling. She didn't have to. When Ryder had helped her rinse her hair there had been a connection between them that was inexplicable. And amazing. And other perceptions she wasn't willing to name or explore. Moreover, he had clearly noticed, too.

Staring at herself she swiped on lip gloss. Too bad she couldn't dim the glimmer in her eyes or dull her flaming cheeks. She had always liked Ryder and looked up to him as a consummate professional, but this—this was unexpected.

Was the surprising emotional connection between them something she should nurture or bury? That was a good question. As long as the chief continued to treat her as if she were not special to him, the wisest thing she could do was act detached, as well. This was certainly not the proper time to try to talk to him about it. He already had a full plate and the more she was involved in ongoing incidents, the less likely he was to open up.

Reason told her he cared. Logic insisted he should be worried about anyone who worked too closely with the police force. Underlying doubts insisted that his solicitousness arose from a sense of duty rather than personal concern.

She could live with that assumption more easily than the notion she might be falling for Ryder Hayes. Phoenix saw small kindnesses as a call to abject devotion. Humans were a lot smarter. They—she—was able to think things through and come to sensible conclusions. So, the man had acted tender toward her. So what? He'd have treated anybody who needed help the same. Wouldn't he?

Sophie had no idea but she was sure she had dawdled in front of the mirror too long already. Tucking her damp hair behind her ears she straightened and gave herself a strict assessment. Her professional face was on. Her clothes were clean. And the bandage on her forehead was still in place.

"Good to go."

Yet she failed to move. Ryder was out there, waiting for her. Could she maintain her firm facade once she rejoined him?

Placing both palms on the vanity she looked

into her own eyes. "I can do this. I *will* do this. I'm just feeling needy because I was scared, that's all."

Assuming anything else was not only foolish, it demonstrated weakness. The part of her life in which she was a victim had ended long ago. She was a grown woman. A strong woman. She could stand on her own two feet and face anything.

"God willing."

Now that she was an adult it was easy to accept that she was stronger and more self-assured. The idea that was hard to swallow was that she was not indestructible. Nobody was. Not even cops in bulletproof vests.

That thought took her straight back to the night her partner, Wes, had died so needlessly. Where had God been then?

Immediately contrite and asking forgiveness from her heavenly Father, Sophie turned and headed for the front door. There were many events in life that seemed wrong, unfair, even cruel, yet if she failed to trust God she'd have nothing.

Faith could be a tenuous thing, particularly when a person was mired in difficulties that seemed inescapable. But a world without faith, without God, was too terrible, too frightening to even contemplate. To her, it would be akin to diving into a pitch-black sea of despair with no chance of return, nothing to grab onto for survival.

If she did not believe in heaven she could not have faced death daily as a patrol officer or trained the dogs those officers counted on for their own well-being.

And speaking of officers… Sophie joined Ryder on the porch, locked her door behind her and let him escort her to his car without argument. They had both reverted to their professional personas and the wall around her heart was firmly in place.

Good. She scanned the street as he did the same. They were a team and they were good at what they did. Sooner or later they'd uncover a clue to her attacker. Or they'd locate Carrie and blame it all on her, a result Sophie preferred over the likelihood that Wes's brother was behind the attacks. The time was coming when she was going to have to break down and tell Ryder about the funeral and she dreaded having to remember, let alone talk about Stan's vitriolic rant.

Sophie stifled a shiver and cast a sidelong glance at Ryder to see if he'd noticed. He apparently had not. That was good, because the last thing she wanted was for him to realize that the more she searched for her shooter, the more she imagined danger behind every tree, every fence, every car.

The basic drawback was not that she was paranoid. The problem was that she had strong cause to be. Somewhere out there was an unfired bullet with her name on it. She had escaped so far. How much longer could she hope to do so?

SEVEN

The weary expression on Louise Donaldson's face told Ryder she and Sophie had not managed to link anyone on the list of suspects to the recent crimes.

He paused by the desk. "Well?"

Both women shook their heads. "I've put the names through our state databases and just accessed FBI," Louise said. "It's not looking promising."

"What about you?" Ryder asked Sophie. "Have you thought of any more names?"

When she shook her head, she averted her gaze the way a guilty suspect might. He didn't like that. "Look at me."

She raised her hazel gaze to meet his blue one. That was all it took for him to be certain she was keeping secrets. He clenched his teeth, jaw muscles working, and tried to stare her down. She didn't yield. Nor did she look away again. If anything, her resolve seemed to strengthen.

"Are you sure?"

Although she failed to voice her reply she did nod.

"All right. Keep searching. I'm going to check with state troopers and ask if they've had any sightings of Carrie. In spite of the rifle, I still think she's our most likely suspect."

"I agree," Sophie said, getting to her feet. "I need a break. How would you like to do a little training with Phoenix this morning? He's really coming around. His attitude is better even after the shooting incident in the yard."

"How about you?"

She smiled and his rigid persona nearly faltered. "Me? I'm always ready to play with dogs."

"I was referring to your head wound."

"Oh, that. I told you I just banged my head. I have a headache, that's all."

"Yeah, I have a headache, too," Ryder muttered, glancing at her and frowning. "Her name is Sophie."

She chuckled low. "Funny. I named my headache Ralph."

"Who's Ralph?"

This time she laughed more loudly. "It's a joke, Chief. Lighten up, will you?"

"Not until Carrie Dunleavy is behind bars."

"I want her caught, too," Sophie said, "but that doesn't mean life can't go on. I have dogs to train and refresher courses to give until we can resume our regular classes. You're here, I'm here, Phoenix is in a run out back. Can you think of a more opportune time to get in a short session with him?"

"I suppose not." Ryder glanced at his office. Titus's bushy Lab tail was sticking out from behind the desk where he was napping. "I'd like to get the dogs acquainted, too, once we decide for sure if the Aussie is staying. Titus can be pretty protective, particularly of Lily."

"That's pack instinct," Sophie told him. "Lily's the littlest member of your family so he guards her."

"Which may be another good reason for him to stay home with her instead of coming to work, but my babysitter is a cat lady."

"We can overcome that problem," Sophie assured him. "I'll need to work with Lily, too, since you won't be at the babysitter's with her. I can give her a few simple commands and Titus will behave for her."

"Tell that to Opal Mullins the first time he bites a cat," Ryder said cynically.

Sophie chuckled again. "Unless she's had them declawed they should be able to fend him off. Anyway, don't borrow trouble. There's enough around already."

"You can say that again."

"Don't borrow trouble, there's…"

Ryder glared at her. "I wasn't being literal, Ms.

Williams. You go get the dog ready. I'll meet you over there in a few."

As she started to walk away he called after her, "And wear a vest. That's an order."

He could tell by the arch of her eyebrows that she was considering an argument even before she said, "If I die of heatstroke it will be your fault."

"I'll take my chances."

And then she was gone. Ryder felt as if all the light had left the squad room. If anything happened to Sophie he knew he'd feel the loss deeply. Would it be the same as losing Melanie. No. Not yet at any rate. But the potential was there. He could sense it.

His late wife had been grounded, sensible, cautious and still had been murdered. How much worse was it for a woman like Sophie; someone who laughed at danger and made fun of his precautions?

The idea of telling her to leave town had occurred to him more than once. She wouldn't, of course. He didn't have to present the plan to know she'd reject it. Was she truly brave or was her stubbornness a by-product of the turbulent childhood she'd mentioned briefly? Perhaps even she didn't know.

Grabbing a bulletproof vest from his office he slipped it on over his uniform shirt and headed for the training complex. One goal was firm in his mind. He was going to get Sophie to tell him what she was hiding; who she had left off the list she'd compiled.

There wasn't a shred of doubt in Ryder's mind. Somewhere in her past lay another suspect. His biggest worry was why she had failed to disclose pertinent information. What was she hiding? And why?

Bright sun made Sophie squint as she stepped outside with Phoenix. Heat radiated off the pavement so she headed straight for what little grass they had managed to keep alive all summer and plopped down in the shade of one of the training obstacles.

She had complied with Ryder's order to wear a vest but had not fastened it tightly around her torso. Having it on was bad enough without cutting off air circulation, too. Besides, it was ugly. Not that she was worried about fashion, she countered. But ever since she'd been forced into more and more proximity with Ryder she'd started to notice when she needed lipstick or when her hair was tousled.

Reminded of his kindness when she'd been trying to wash her hair, she lightly touched the bandage at her temple. The cut barely hurt although there was a raised, bruised area around it.

"Better that than a bullet hole," she muttered, feeling a shiver shoot up her spine despite the

August heat. Lying beside her, Phoenix raised his head.

"I'm okay, boy," Sophie told him. She stroked his head and scratched behind his ears, enjoying the velvety feel of the fine, gray-and-white hair. If she hadn't been waiting for the chief to join them she might have laid her head on the dog's back and closed her eyes. Animals, especially canines, affected her that way. Being around them was calming, relaxing to the point of almost dozing off when she let herself stop working long enough.

"Here I am," she whispered pensively, "in a place I thought was perfect until we discovered Carrie Dunleavy had been killing off her competition and any guy who had the misfortune to resemble the chief."

Slowly shaking her head she found she was still coming to grips with the truth. How could she—how could all of them—have missed the signs of the police department secretary's mental unbalance and hidden agenda? How, indeed?

"Because she never made waves," Sophie concluded. "She baked us cookies, she was always willing to take on extra work and help out, she was everything and yet nothing."

That was probably the crux of the problem, Sophie concluded. Nobody really took Carrie seriously. If they noticed her at all it was to ask her to do more work. Socially, she was disconnected despite her efforts at ingratiation via food or little gifts to selected people.

In a way, Sophie felt sorry for the woman. She understood feelings of alienation. They had nearly destroyed her during adolescence. If it had not been for turning her fractured life over to God, to Jesus, she didn't know how she'd have survived.

And speaking of survival... She spotted Ryder crossing the distance between them. The brim of his cap shaded his eyes but she could already tell he was a man on a mission. Hopefully, his goal was to train a dog, because if he intended to keep probing into her past she was not going to be a happy camper.

Instead of smiling or greeting her verbally, he stopped at her feet and dropped something small and light into her lap.

She started to thank him until she realized what it was—a package of chewing gum with a blue wrapper!

Sophie did exactly what Ryder had expected. She picked up the gum and stared at it.

"Is this anything like what you say you saw in your yard?" he asked.

"It's exactly like the trash in the yard, only this is new and the other was unwrapped." Wide-eyed, she looked up at him. "Where did you find it?"

"In a box in the station," he said. "Carrie's personal items were checked for evidence tying her to the murders, then stored. I thought I remembered seeing something blue like that package of gum. When you said you vaguely remembered the same thing, I decided to look."

Color left Sophie's cheeks. "*She* was the one outside my house?"

"Possibly. Can you think of any other reason someone might have been watching you?" He crouched in front of her, willing her to open up to him. Because she began to slowly shake her head he raised a hand. "Stop. Don't insult me by denying it. You and I both know you're holding back information. I just can't decide if it's because you don't trust me or because you think you can handle the situation by yourself."

"It's neither." Sophie sighed deeply. "I guess it's an old loyalty. One person made serious threats but that was years ago. I can't imagine Stan still blaming me for his brother's death."

"He wasn't on your list, was he?"

"No." She began to pluck blades of dry grass and crush them between her fingertips. "Stan Allen is the brother of my late partner, Wes. He accosted me at the cemetery after the funeral. At the time, I thought Stan was going to hit me. He might have if my fellow officers hadn't pulled him away."

"Have you heard from him since?"

"No. We both left Mesa. I went one direction,

and he went another. I never would have thought of him if you hadn't kept pressing me."

"All right." Holding out a hand to her, Ryder pulled her to her feet. "Here's what we'll do. First, I want you to tell Louise everything you know about this guy. Then use your own sources to try to track him down while she checks databases. Call old friends in Mesa. Whatever you have to do. Just find him."

Sophie held up the pack of gum. "What do you want me to do with this?"

"Put it on your desk where you'll see it every day."

"Why? If Stan is my stalker, what difference does it make what kind of gum Carrie liked?"

"It doesn't. I'm hoping it will become a symbol and remind you to be more cautious."

"No matter who is after me, you mean?"

Ryder's jaw clenched. "Exactly."

Sophie managed to accomplish everything the chief had told her to do, plus introduce Titus to Phoenix without incident. The older dog seemed unconcerned about the energetic Aussie, particularly because Phoenix practically tiptoed once he realized the senior Lab was boss. Not only was there no challenge for dominance, Phoenix flopped down in front of Titus and rolled onto his back, the recognized canine signal for surrender.

Sophie was seated on the cool floor, legs folded, when Ryder came back into his office.

"You were supposed to be looking for info on Stan Allen."

"I was. I found him. Or, rather, Louise did."

"And?"

"And, his last known address was an apartment near Flagstaff. Louise called the building manager. Stan still rents there but she says she hasn't seen him for weeks."

"Uh-oh. Any idea where he went or why?"

"No. I've been giving it some thought, though, and I can see a reason why he might have decided to come after me at this late date."

Ryder perched on the edge of his desk and looked down at her. "Go on."

"The news. When you uncovered Carrie's crimes, this department made all the papers and TV news. They published lots of pictures and all our names, at one time or another. If Stan recognized me, maybe that's what set him off."

"Logical," Ryder told her. He circled his desk and picked up the phone. "I'll check with Mesa's chief and fill him in on our suspicions. We can get the state troopers involved as soon as we know a little more."

"You mean as soon as you catch Stan trying to kill me again?" She couldn't help sounding sarcastic. "Sorry. I know there's no proof. It just seems possible."

Ryder scowled at her. "Yes, it does. Think of how much closer to answers we might be if you'd given us his name sooner."

She knew he was right, yet felt compelled to defend her decision. "I am responsible for his brother's death. I didn't see any reason to cause him further trouble if he was innocent, so I held back."

It surprised her when Ryder quickly circled his desk and grabbed her shoulders. "Let me explain something to you, Ms. Williams. Criminals who shoot cops are the guilty ones. They make the decision to fire, not you."

"I should have seen it coming. Warned him."

"And if you had, he might still have died. Nobody knows why these things happen. It's so unfair it makes me want to scream at God but that doesn't do any good."

He paused and Sophie could tell he was struggling to continue. When he said, "I know. I did that when Melanie was murdered," Sophie wanted to weep for him. So much pain. So much suffering that continued to haunt him.

Her voice was soft, barely audible, when she said, "I can still see Wes in that dark alley, falling and just lying there."

"And I see my wife on the path where she died, but I make an effort to remember the other times, the good times. There were plenty of those if I choose to call up the sweet memories. You need to do that. And stop blaming yourself for what happened. It will only hurt you."

Did she dare voice her innermost thoughts? Was this the right time? Given Ryder's efforts to temper her own lingering guilt she decided to speak her mind.

"That's good advice," Sophie said gently, meeting his blue gaze bravely. "Have you taken it, yourself?"

He abruptly released her shoulders and stepped back. "I don't know what you mean."

"Yes, you do. You have always blamed yourself for letting Melanie walk home that night. Everybody knows it. And now that we know Carrie killed her you're probably thinking you should have seen the symptoms of her mental instability, but none of us did. You are no more responsible for the senseless attack on your wife than I am for Wes's. If you want me to stop feeling guilty, I think you'd better do the same."

He turned his back to her. Sophie could tell how close he was to breaking down so she silently left the office, closing the door behind her. Healing of a broken heart was a lot like doing surgery on a real one; sometimes you had to cause more pain in order to effect a return to life and health.

What about herself? Suppose the repeated attacks on her had been Stan's doing? If so, he believed he had good reason and for that she still could not blame him. She wasn't going to be foolish and expose herself to his anger, if that were the case, but she couldn't help wishing he was innocent.

On her way through the main office she was stopped by Louise Donaldson. "We got some info on a print in that black car your perp left behind in the street."

Sophie brightened. "Carrie?"

"Nope." Louise shook her head. "It came back as unidentified in local databases so I sent it to IAFIS."

"It wasn't Carrie's?" Touching the small bandage on her temple at the memory, she winced.

"No. Sorry. I'll keep trying."

"Okay. Thanks." What else could she say? If Stan had been a police officer like his brother they'd have his prints. The same went for the military. Since Wes had never mentioned much about his younger brother she was at a loss. All she did recall was how worried her late partner had been about his only sibling committing petty crimes and perhaps starting down the wrong path in life.

Had Stan graduated to felonies? If so, his fingerprints should be on file, assuming he'd been arrested and charged.

And if he hadn't? What if he had been hardened by a life of minor crimes and was just now progressing to one that could prove deadly? To her?

That notion was enough to set her nerves on

edge and keep them there, as if danger lay around the next corner or hid behind every closed door.

In truth, it did.

EIGHT

Passing days seemed to drag. With no more threats to anyone and no sightings of a woman resembling Carrie, even Ryder began to relax a little.

He'd spent some time with Sophie while training Phoenix and was starting to see what the dog was capable of. He was an excellent tracker, even with distractions that might throw off most dogs. And he got along with Titus, another plus in his favor. That was why, when Sophie suggested he take both dogs home with him, he wasn't too surprised.

"You think he's ready for that?" Ryder asked.

"If I come along and make sure he and Lily are okay together. She's used to a dog that lazes around a lot. It's going to be different to have one that wants to play all the time."

"Will it spoil him?"

"Not if you never let her take charge when he's in his working vest and on leash." She smiled, making Ryder wonder if the air-conditioning in his office had failed. "It was the same with Titus," she reminded him.

"I know. But he was already used to me by the time Lily started to walk. He let her hang on him when she was just learning to stand. I should have taken pictures. It was really cute to see the two of them together."

"Well, now you'll have three. What time do you want me to have him ready?"

Ryder eyed the two dogs lying beneath his desk. Titus had claimed the prime spot in the back of the kneehole while Phoenix shared as best he could. "What do you have to do to get him ready? Pack his bags?"

That made Sophie's smile widen to a grin. Ryder ran a finger under his collar.

"Don't let on, but I'm giving him a bath and a pedicure. While I'm at it I'll do Titus, too, since they're such buddies."

"Well, don't forget his toothbrush," Ryder quipped. "I know for a fact that Titus hates to share."

She nodded. "I know you're kidding but I really will include separate toys for each dog. I don't want Titus to think he has to fight for the ones at home. Actually, it might be wise for you to gather them up at first."

"Okay. Anything else?"

"Not that I can think of, other than making sure

Titus doesn't try to protect Lily. That's one of the reasons I want to be there."

Ryder noted the fondness in her expression when she looked at Phoenix. "You could keep him a while longer," he suggested. "It won't hurt, will it?"

"Only if he gets too attached to me."

"Or you get too attached to him? I can tell he's a favorite."

"Which is another reason I need to pass him on to you," Sophie admitted. "I can't tell you how proud I am of his progress, and of him. He's a really great K-9."

"Thanks to you," Ryder said. "I'll phone Opal and tell her we're picking up Lily early today. Do you want to ride with me or drive separately?"

Again, Sophie's grin lit up his office. "Separately. Definitely. Now that I have my SUV back I want to use it."

Seeking to ease his own concerns about her, he joked, "Just see that you don't park it in the middle of another gunfight, will you?"

She mimicked a salute. "Yes, sir."

Ryder waved her off, managing to keep smiling until she'd gone. Recent peace in Desert Valley had given them all a respite, but he knew their problems weren't over.

This period was akin to the lull before a storm that brought flash floods to the arroyos and swept away anybody who was thoughtless enough to be caught in the wrong place at the wrong time.

He gazed out at a clear blue sky, imagining the seeds of black, roiling clouds just over the horizon. Even when the sun was shining and the air still, the only thing a desert dweller could be certain of was that when the rains did come, they would arrive as a deluge.

So would the danger that was temporarily on hold, Ryder told himself. Until they had Carrie Dunleavy and perhaps Stan Allen in custody, nobody was safe.

Particularly not Sophie.

Sophie was taken aback when the chief approached her to suggest a change of plans. She was also barefoot and knee-deep in a dog-washing project. When she straightened to speak with him, Phoenix shook, sending blobs of suds flying.

She blew her hair out of her eyes and flung shampoo off her hands. "Phew! That was fun. Take off your shoes and jump right in."

"No, thanks. Is it safe to get soap in the cut on your head?"

"That's all healed. I'm fine."

"Good. I was just thinking."

"Clever plan. Wandering aimlessly isn't productive." She chuckled at her own lame joke.

"I'm serious. I think you should keep Phoenix with you until we have your shooter in custody."

"You must be kidding. I don't do all this for fun—although it is—I do it because I want to help law enforcement. That does not include making pets of working dogs."

"I know, but…"

Leaving the dog tied to keep him from running off, Sophie released the water spray nozzle and faced the chief. "But, nothing. This is my job. Let me do it."

"I wasn't trying to stop you. I just thought you'd appreciate having a watchdog in your house at night."

"If I feel I need a watchdog I can always take one of the younger dogs home with me. I've had my eye on those shepherds we got from Marian Foxcroft six months ago."

"You're serious?"

"Of course I am." Truthfully, Sophie had had to force herself to arrange to relinquish Phoenix. That was the main reason she was sticking to her decision. Every day she spent with him was one more day to love him more. If a person and a dog could be said to be soul mates, she and the Aussie were. He seemed in tune with her, and she with him. That kind of bond had occurred in the past, of course, but not often.

"All right. Have it your way." Ryder started to turn away, then looked over his shoulder long enough to point to the sudsy, dripping dog. "You missed a spot."

Sophie knew she shouldn't listen to the urging of her mischievous side. Before she had a chance to talk herself out of it, however, she grabbed the handle of the spray nozzle and squeezed. A spurt of warm water hit Ryder between the shoulder blades. *Splat!*

He shouted. The look of astonishment on his face when he whirled, hands up in self-defense and eyes wide, was priceless. Sophie wasn't sure which of them was most shocked; him for being hit or her for spraying him.

Everybody froze. Gina peeked around the corner from the kennel area. Her mouth gaped. Sophie laughed until tears dripped down her already-damp cheeks.

Not Ryder. He slowly stepped away, removed his watch, took off his belt with the holster and laid it aside, too. Then he bent to untie the dress shoes he wore instead of boots when he expected to spend the day in his office. Those went on the seat of a stool to keep them off the floor surrounding the open shower and dog-bathing area.

Sophie watched, incredulous, as he started toward her, arms extended as if he were entering a wrestling match.

"Uh-oh. Sorry, Chief. I don't know what came over me. My brain must have skipped a beat." She backed up, nozzle at the ready. "Stop! Don't make me use this."

She heard a growl. It was Phoenix. The last

thing she wanted was for the dog to bite Ryder to protect her so she commanded him to stay and stepped away, making sure his leash was tied tightly.

Grasping the nozzle with both hands and taking a shooter's stance she shouted, "Don't come any closer. I'm warning you."

Someone in the doorway let out a whoop. In the few moments it took Sophie to check who was there, Ryder charged for the closest other hose nozzle.

Instinct tightened Sophie's grip. The blast of water hit him in profile. He didn't falter. Instead, he grabbed the separate hose, took aim and returned fire.

Sophie was ducking, screeching and laughing hysterically. Any stream that didn't meet its equal between them hit her hard. Shutting her eyes she tried to regain enough balance to fight back but it was futile. He was dousing her while the rookies in the impromptu audience cheered and applauded. Even Louise got in the spirit of the water fight when she yelled, "Soak her good, Chief."

"Ack. Eeek. Phooey." Phoenix had shaken enough suds in her direction that she could taste soap.

All the fight left her at about the same time Ryder stopped spraying. She staggered back against the wall of the shower. Water streamed from her hair, swirling down the floor drain with the soap from the dog.

Sophie gasped for breath. Saw his larger, strong hands resting on the tile beside her. She might look like a drowned pup but he was far from dry himself.

A sidelong glance proved to her that he was no longer feeling playful. He straightened and addressed the watching crowd.

"If anybody mentions this incident outside the office or I hear even a hint of rumor on the street, you will *all* be in deep trouble. Got it?"

Multiple versions of "Yes, sir. Yes, Chief," echoed and faded away as the parties dispersed, leaving Sophie and Ryder alone with Phoenix.

She faced him with enough smile to hopefully prove she wasn't mad but not so much he'd think she was mocking him. Leaning to one side she twisted her long hair to wring it out. "Well, that was different."

"You shouldn't start something you can't finish," he grumbled.

Hesitating to assess his expression, she decided he wasn't truly angry. "I thought I did fairly well. You'll have to go home to change."

"I have a clean uniform in my locker."

"Oh."

"Did you ever replace the clothing in yours?"

"Not with good clothes. I brought stuff to

change into when I was doing something messy, like washing a dog."

Ryder eyed her soggy self. "You already changed?"

"Nope. That would make too much sense. Besides, I was in a hurry to get Phoenix all spiffed up for you."

"Well, you may as well finish before you dry off." One eyebrow arched. "I'm going to turn my back and walk away now. Don't get any funny ideas."

"Who, me?"

"Yes, you."

There was no impishness left in her after their playful tussle. In its place were surprise and joy and an all-over sense of relief from the tension that had been plaguing them all.

Sophie smiled to herself as she returned to her dog-washing chore. "That's what we should do during the street fair instead of a dunking booth," she told Phoenix. "We should organize a good old-fashioned water fight and invite the whole town to take part."

The soggy dog didn't act impressed. He hung his head as she carefully rinsed and toweled him before taking him out into the sunshine. Dry desert air did the rest.

Sophie's hair was almost dry, too, by the time she returned to the training center to give Titus his bath.

The old dog plodded into the shower room obediently and stood still while she shampooed him. "What a good boy. You're better behaved than I am," she cooed.

From somewhere in the hallway came a familiar voice. "You can say that again."

Sophie had to smile. "Which part?" she called back, "the 'good boy' or the 'better behaved'?"

It didn't surprise her that Ryder chose to not answer. Losing control and becoming playful the way he had when she'd sprayed him had to be terribly embarrassing. If anyone else had tried the same thing they'd probably have been reprimanded for insubordination.

But not her. Not this time. How long had it been since that man had felt comfortable enough to play with anyone besides his little girl? Probably years.

Sophie felt immensely blessed. Even if nothing more came of their relaxed friendship after Carrie was apprehended, at least they had shared a little enjoyment today.

And, she suddenly realized, Ryder wasn't the only one lacking fun in his life. She was just as bad. The cares of the days, the threats of violence, had usurped the place of simple pleasures. Yes, they needed to be vigilant. But they also needed to remember to live. That amounted to more than merely stopping to smell the roses. It had to be based in thankfulness for what they had been given and backed up by faith in the One who had blessed them.

Funny how that was a lot easier to think about than to put into practice, particularly when being shot at.

Lily was ecstatic when her daddy told her they were finally going to bring Phoenix home. Climbing out of the car as soon as Ryder parked, she bounced on her toes waiting for Sophie to bring her new playmate.

Ryder let Titus out, as planned, and watched Sophie leash Phoenix before telling him to jump down. So far, so good. Titus had wandered off to sniff the yard and paid no attention, even when Lily launched herself at the Australian shepherd and gave his ruff a hug.

"He smells good," the child said. "Like lemons."

"That's because I gave him a bath," Sophie said with a sideways glance at Ryder. "Your daddy helped."

He knew he was blushing when he scowled back at her. Why he had acted like a kid was beyond him. What had felt okay at the time now seemed outlandish and totally unacceptable. Of course it was. He had a position of authority to maintain. Chief officers did not go around having water fights with staff. It didn't really matter that as head K-9 trainer, Sophie didn't work for him.

They functioned as part of the same team and had always treated each other as equals. At least he had. By spraying him, she had proved otherwise.

Ryder knew he should be furious but for some reason he wasn't. After all, he could have walked away despite the obvious challenge. There was just something about Sophie that had insisted he retaliate.

"I wanna play hide-'n-seek," Lily said.

"In the house. Not out here," Sophie replied.

Ryder led the way, opened the front door of his ranch house and ushered them all inside. He had a woman who came to clean once a week and Lily was good about picking up her toys, so he wasn't embarrassed about any clutter except the dog toys scattered in the living room. "Hold on a second. I'll pick up after Titus."

"It may be all right," Sophie said, eyeing the old dog. "He's not acting possessive at all. The time together in your office has helped a lot."

"All they did was sleep," Ryder countered. "Speaking of which, look."

Titus had already curled up in his favorite spot on the sofa and laid his chin on his front paws, relaxed but watching Lily.

"Don't forget what I told you on the way home." Ryder made sure he had his daughter's attention. "You can't just play with Phoenix or Titus will be sad. You have to give them both lots of love."

"I know." She darted to the couch, planted a

smooch on the yellow Lab's broad nose, then dashed back to Phoenix and Sophie. "You hold him while I hide, okay?"

"Okay. I'll help him count to ten."

The sweet, agreeable way Sophie handled Lily warmed Ryder's heart. Adults often tended to belittle or ignore children but not Sophie. She was as in tune with Lily as she was with the dogs she trained. Maybe that was what he found so attractive. She had a natural way of behaving and accepting things that made her easy to like.

And lowered his defenses, he added, chagrined. The vivid memories of holding her under the spray with water going everywhere and her screaming like a kid kept popping into his mind. If word that he'd tried to drown the head trainer ever got out he'd never live it down.

"Ten!" Sophie called out. The instant she released Phoenix he was on Lily's trail. So was Titus. They rounded the corner into the hallway, nails scrambling on the hardwood floor.

Lily was giggling by the time Ryder and Sophie reached the spot where the dogs were. Phoenix had his head and shoulders under the bed. Titus was down on his front paws, rear in the air, tail wagging in circles.

"Looks like they found her," Ryder said.

Sophie was laughing. "I guess so. Where's his reward toy?"

"Around here somewhere." Ryder shrugged.

"Sorry. I know I'm supposed to stick to training protocol but sometimes when they're playing I forget."

"It's okay. Lily can be their reward. Neither of them is wearing his vest so technically they're not working."

Sobering, Ryder eyed her. "Neither are you."

"Give me a break. It's hot outside and we haven't had any trouble for a week or so. I don't need to run around in body armor all the time."

"You should. We both know it."

The roll of her eyes was not the least bit comforting. He knew she wasn't a fool, yet she continued to defy logic.

All he could hope for, pray for, was that if and when the unknown menace struck again, his or her aim would be as bad as it had been in the past.

Unfortunately, that wasn't a given. Fire enough shots and sooner or later, one of them was likely to hit its mark.

NINE

Leaving Phoenix behind with Ryder wasn't nearly as hard on Sophie as going home alone turned out to be. Her house was dark, the front yard illuminated only by a distant streetlight. She parked the SUV so its headlights would shine on the back porch, then hurried inside before the automatic system shut them off.

So quiet. So lonely. So empty. She ate a solitary supper of leftover tuna fish on wheat bread, then tidied up the kitchen before heading for bed with a good book. It was times like these when she almost wished she had a permanent pet like a cat. Almost. If she could find one with the temperament of a dog she might consider it. In the meantime, she'd have to be content to foster her trainees, even if that did mean eventually letting them go.

The pages on the paperback soon blurred and she began to nod. Just before falling asleep she switched off the bedside light. Her dreams were filled with myriad dogs. And one man. He stood afar, his face in shadow, yet she knew it was Ryder Hayes as surely as she knew… That noise in the background was out of place.

Staying very still, Sophie opened her eyes. Nothing was moving. There was no unusual sound coming from anywhere, inside or outside. A dog would have been able to tell instantly if she should be afraid, of course, and she'd always believed anything a canine tried to tell her. Too bad she was on her own tonight.

A glance at the bedside clock showed three in the morning. Darkness would have been complete if not for a waxing moon. Sophie knew she should forget the rude awakening and go back to sleep but her heart was still beating too fast and her eyes refused to shut.

They were adjusting to seeing in the dimness when she heard glass shatter. A window? A drinking glass hitting the floor in her kitchen? It didn't matter. All she knew was that her home was being violated. She was not going to simply lie there and act the victim.

There was no time for a robe over her long gown, at least not until she was armed and ready. Scooping up her cell phone she slipped the revolver out of its holster and headed for the walk-in closet, easing the door closed behind her. Walls and doors weren't bulletproof, despite what TV and movies showed. They were, however, good hiding places. If no one could see her they wouldn't know to shoot.

Her hands were shaking. And the cell phone beeped when she pushed the call button. Sophie was hesitant to speak after that. Listening for footsteps she cradled the phone, only then remembering to send up a frantic prayer.

"Nine-one-one. What's your emergency?"

Rats, it was Missy Cooper instead of Louise. "This is Sophie Williams on Second Street. I have a prowler. In my house!"

"Can you get out and go to a neighbor's?"

"No."

"I'm sorry, ma'am. You'll have to speak up. I can barely hear you."

"Tell you what, Missy," Sophie almost hissed. "You can send help or leave the guy to me. I'm armed and will shoot if I have to."

"Units are on the way," the dispatcher said.

That's more like it. Sophie broke the connection. She knew the phone would continue to beep while she navigated to silent mode so she buried it under a pile of blankets in the hopes it wouldn't make any more noise.

Then she eased open the closet door and peeked out the thin slit. At first there was nothing. Then she heard a slow, steady series of footsteps. Someone was trying to sneak in by tiptoeing.

She was about to ease the door closed again when she heard the metallic swish and click of the slide on an automatic pistol. The shooter chambered a bullet.

Never before had it been this hard to hold perfectly still. Shaking to the core, she leaned on the doorknob for stability. The hinges squeaked.

Sophie stifled a gasp, returned both hands to her own gun and raised it, ready to fire.

A shadow fell over her bed. Watching it, she realized she'd thrown aside her light comforter rather than turn the air-conditioning down too low and had left behind a raised ridge of bedclothes that resembled a body.

The prowler took aim. All she could see were his hands and the barrel of the gun but she knew it was a man. She gritted her teeth, anticipating earsplitting noise. When he fired, the blast shook the windows.

The muzzle flash was temporarily blinding. The temptation to shoot back was great, but unless she could actually tell who and what she was shooting at she wasn't going to fire. Besides, he still didn't know he hadn't shot her in the bed and it would be foolish to give away her position.

Distant sirens made beautiful night music. Sophie heard her attacker running down the hall. A door slammed. That was *not* enough to draw her out of hiding. She wasn't going to move until she saw a police badge, preferably worn by one of the rookies she had trained, or, even better, by a certain chief she happened to be unduly fond of.

The sirens wound down, then stopped. Boots clomped down the hallway. She heard officers hollering, "Clear," as they checked the front of the house.

Releasing the cocked hammer on her own gun, Sophie was finally able to breathe.

She shouted, "In here," then slid to the floor to sit and wait because her bones felt as if they'd been left on the dash of a hot car in the Arizona summer sun and had melted into useless puddles like a box of wax crayons.

Scared? Sure. But it was more than that. She'd been less afraid of losing her own life than she was of being forced to take someone else's.

That was not a good sign.

Ryder had ordered Officer Tristan McKeller to stay with Lily when the rookie had brought the message about the attack on Sophie. They'd been unable to reach him because Lily had been tinkering with Ryder's pager and had shut off his cell phone, as well. Tristan had been chosen to check on the chief since his K-9, Jesse, was trained to pinpoint arson, not track humans.

What Ryder wanted to do first was set eyes on Sophie and see for himself that she was okay. He took the stairs to her front porch at a run, then halted a few feet short of sweeping her into his arms when they came face-to-face. Neither of them moved for several seconds. Finally he asked, "You all right?"

She nodded. "Yes, but I need a new bedcover. Mine has a bullet hole in it." Glancing past him she asked, "Did you bring the dogs?"

"Yes. Both of them. I wasn't sure if Titus could last long enough, and we don't want to lose this trail."

"Shane was first on scene," Sophie told him. "I think he's got the area around the house covered."

Ryder's feet were still planted and so were hers. "I should go."

Sophie nodded. He reluctantly left her and joined the operation in progress.

"We have dogs deployed in three directions," Shane reported. "Do you want to take command, Chief?"

"You're doing fine. I'd rather be tracking."

"Okay. The only area that hasn't been checked yet is the open field on the other side of the fence behind her house."

"We can take that," Ryder told him. "I brought both dogs. I'll leave Titus for backup and start with Phoenix. It's pretty rough walking out there. I don't want to tax Titus if I don't have to."

"Agreed," Shane spoke into his radio, then nodded at Ryder. "All set. They know you're coming. I'd hate to have one of the other rookies make a mistake and take a potshot at you."

"So would I. Do we have a description?"

"Big guy. Probably dressed in dark clothing. That's about it."

"No chance it's Carrie?"

"Not this time," the officer said.

In a way, Ryder was glad. If Carrie wasn't after Sophie, that meant the extra time he'd spent with the trainer had not been at fault.

He smiled faintly as he prepared Phoenix and donned his own bulletproof vest. It also meant it would be safer to spend time with Sophie once this was over.

Nothing sounded better—except capturing whoever had tried to kill her tonight. He set his jaw and drove around the block, more than ready to track down the assailant.

Left behind, Sophie was far more nervous than she would have been if she'd been taking part in the search. Granted, it was no longer her job to go into the field with the dogs she trained but she really wanted to break the rules now and then.

There was plenty of activity in her yard to keep her interested, yet all she could think about was Ryder—and Phoenix. She approached Shane Weston. "All clear around here?"

He smiled and gave her a casual salute. "Yes, ma'am. Your place has been cleared and we have dogs searching the neighbors' yards."

Satisfied by the report she stepped out onto her back porch and paused to scan the darkness. Headlights swept the distant street where no houses blocked her view. A vehicle came to a stop, red lights spinning. A floodlight played over the desert terrain before someone—Ryder—brought Phoenix out of the back of the patrol car.

Sophie didn't have to see clearly to know who was out there and what he was doing. Instead of using a flashlight and making himself an easy target, Ryder let the dog bring him to the bare ground and sniff around.

One of her main concerns was snakes, like before. This time of year they were only active at night and this was the perfect time to stumble across one. If the chief hadn't been working a dog she would have had a lot more concern. That was the great thing about K-9s. Their keen senses more than made up for a human's lack.

Peering into the hazard-filled night, Sophie was reminded to pray. She certainly had while hiding in her closet, she recalled, although not one word had stuck in her memory. That was the trouble with frantic prayer. It came in a rush of fear rather than organized thought. And, she concluded, it was the kind that sped straight to heaven because it wasn't all cluttered up with a person's ego or foolishness.

"Thank You, Jesus," she whispered, truly grateful for her escape and for the men and women who had come to search for the would-be assassin. Especially one man.

A shout echoed. Her hands tightened on the railing at the edge of the small porch.

Suddenly, the rear yard was filled with running figures and barking dogs. Another dog barked in the distance. If that was Phoenix, he'd certainly recovered his courage. His bark sounded a lot more menacing than ever before.

People were yelling. Sophie tried to ask rookie James Harrison for details as he passed, but the baying of his bloodhound, Hawk, drowned her out.

The melee stopped at the back fence. Some of the officers were playing lights over the scrub brush and rocks dotting the field.

"There! There he is. Eleven o'clock from my position."

Judging by his bark, Phoenix had to be coming at a run and Ryder with him. Five flashlights zeroed in on the unknown man.

Shots cut through the darkness. Sophie instinctively ducked and stayed in a crouch. She was not going to hide inside. Not when so much was going on out there. Not when her friends and colleagues were taking fire.

"Jesus, help Ryder," she prayed. "Keep him safe." As far as she was concerned, his survival far outweighed the capture of her deadly stalker.

The officers at the fence began to cheer. That was more than Sophie could take. She had to join them.

Two shadows were grappling in the field. Phoenix had the pant leg of one of them in his teeth and was shaking it. The other had to be Ryder.

Sophie could hardly breathe. Hardly think. When a gun fired again she stifled a scream.

The pursuit was almost over. Ryder had launched himself at the quarry as soon as he'd gotten close enough.

The man had whirled and fired but the shot had gone wild when Phoenix had hit him below the knees and taken a bite of his leg.

Ryder left his own gun holstered rather than chance sending a bullet into the officers still at Sophie's. He'd seen them gathering when they'd helped him locate the fleeing criminal and knew the fence would slow them down enough that he'd have to finish this job himself.

He ducked a punch, then landed one of his own before wrapping the shooter in a bear hug and shoving him to the ground.

Phoenix immediately went for the arm holding the gun.

The wiry attacker tried to bring the muzzle to bear on the dog. Ryder was on him too fast. "Drop the gun!"

The captured man shouted curses and thrashed.

"Drop it," Ryder ordered again.

"She killed my brother. She deserves to die," he yelled.

And Ryder knew without a doubt who he had caught. The one person Sophie had left off her list of suspects was the menace after all.

Wrenching the gun from Stan Allen's hand he called off his dog, then rolled the man over and cuffed him.

As Ryder stood and pulled his captive to his feet, a group cheer arose.

"Good job, Chief," someone called. Others agreed.

He listened for Sophie's voice, hoping she had seen how well her dog had worked in a crisis situation. Although he couldn't hear her cheering above the cacophony he was certain she'd be celebrating, too. After all, this meant she could finally relax and start to live her life more normally.

Perhaps, God willing, he could, too, he mused as he led his prisoner back to his car, loaded him and let Phoenix jump into the front for a change.

Closing his eyes, Ryder pictured his darling Melanie. Would she mind if he took Opal's sage advice and began to think of finding a mother for Lily?

Expecting peace and assurance, Ryder was disappointed. It was easy to understand why. With Carrie Dunleavy still at large nobody could really go back to living freely, to enjoying life as it had once been.

"But that day will come," Ryder told himself

with a sigh. He—they—would put an end to Desert Valley's fear and strife, one way or another.

If the state troopers didn't locate Carrie she might even come back to town and give him another crack at catching her.

That thought sent a shiver up his spine. Some witnesses had been positive the shooter at the depot had been a woman. Was it possible they had been so agitated they were mistaken? Maybe. Hopefully. This guy was about the same height as Carrie and had plenty of matching brown hair.

Ryder was looking forward to questioning him and getting him to admit to all the attacks. He'd better. Or they'd have to rethink everything.

TEN

To say Sophie was tired was the understatement of the year. She'd dozed off twice in the meeting Ryder had called at the DVPD the following morning to brief his staff and the dog trainers.

She heard her name and jerked. "Sorry. What?"

"I said we need to work out assignments for the homecoming celebration and street fair. I was planning to pair rookies and dogs with local officials and send them out on regular patrols. Since the fair is only open Friday and Saturday I think we can split the duty without everybody having to work all the time."

"I'd like to take some of the older pups out," Sophie said. "And I know Ellen wants to use the crowd for service dog training, too."

"Will Lee Earnshaw be around? If he is, he can handle some of the dogs for her, maybe in shifts. I'll need her on the street with Carly at least part of the time."

Sophie nodded. "He's going back to vet school,

but he expects to be here for the homecoming."
She had to smile. "He's not too crazy about Desert Valley after spending two years in Canyon County Prison for a crime he didn't commit, but he can't bear to stay away from Ellen."

"I guess that's understandable," Ryder replied, "even though he was exonerated."

"True. And they might never have met if he hadn't been involved in the Prison Pups program."

"Enough personal discussion, Williams. Let's get back to working out a schedule."

She almost snickered at his efforts to act so formal in front of the group. Those who hadn't seen their water fight had surely heard about it. After that, there was little chance she and the chief would be viewed as anything but friends. Which suited her just fine.

"All right," Sophie said, stifling a yawn and stretching her arms overhead. "I'd like to be included, as I said. You can either put me down as a regular or let me float to wherever we need extra coverage." That innocent suggestion brought a grin. "No pun intended. I didn't mean to bring up anything connected to water when I said *float*."

Muted snickers popped up. Ryder's cheeks colored. "That's enough. There will be no more jokes about *water* while I'm chief, is that clear?"

"Yes, sir." Sophie was giggling. "We'll consider the incident with the dog shampoo as *water under the bridge*."

Watching the expressions flashing across his handsome, if somewhat rosy face, she wondered if she'd gone too far. There was a point past which she should not go, if only to preserve the chief's decorum.

She waved both hands. "Sorry. That just slipped out. I'm so happy to be alive and kicking after last night, I guess I'm feeling a little childish."

Ryder seemed to forgive her teasing. "Understandable."

"Is Stan still refusing to talk?"

"Yes. After we brought him in I had Doc Evans look him over and prescribe something to calm him down. We'll have another go at him when he's acting more rational."

Sighing, she let her glance pass over the others in the meeting. "I suppose you all know the story by now. It's not something I'm proud of. Wes Allen, Stan's brother, was a good cop and a good man. He should not have died."

"Lots of people shouldn't have died," Ryder countered. He wasn't exactly frowning but he certainly didn't look happy. Not that Sophie blamed him. If she was having this much trouble getting over losing Wes, how much more difficult must it be for the chief to go on with his life after Melanie's murder?

And this was not the right time for platitudes or scripture quotes. Well-meaning friends and colleagues had bombarded her with what they had considered consolation and had only made her sorrow deeper, her loss more painful. Words had been inadequate then and they still were. The people who had brought the most comfort were the ones who had simply patted her shoulder or offered a hug without comment. Or wept with her later, she added. It had taken her weeks to cry and yet, even now, when she least expected it, some little thing might trigger more tears.

Wishing she had a dog lying at her feet, Sophie clenched her hands together in her lap and fought to appear relaxed. All but one of the people in the room seemed to accept her ruse.

The instant she let her gaze lock with Ryder's she knew she hadn't fooled him. In a strange way, that was comforting. Once again they were silently, unobtrusively, sharing empathy. She could not have accepted his pity any more than he'd have welcomed hers. But this was different. It was a connection she had not sought, yet it existed. Or did it?

Averting her eyes, she began to wonder if this kind of feeling was normal or if she was as deluded as Carrie Dunleavy had been. *Correction, as Carrie still is.*

That conclusion caused Sophie to ask, "What about Carrie? Are we going to have to worry about her crashing the homecoming or have there been reports of sightings elsewhere?"

"State troopers have posted a lot of possibilities," Ryder replied. "Most were in the southern part of the state, around Phoenix." At that, the dozing K-9 at his feet perked up and cocked his head. "No, not you," he said, finally smiling slightly.

That was the way Sophie felt whenever she was accompanied by a dog so she, too, smiled. "Maybe you'd better say Mesa or Tempe."

"Looks like it." Ryder concentrated on Louise. "Try to accommodate everybody when you make up the special duty roster, then bring it to me for approval. McKeller will want to be free enough to leave if Ariel Martin hasn't had her baby by then." Ryder knew that Tristan, one of his rookies, had gotten very close to Ariel, his daughter's teacher, during a case last month. Ariel was nine months pregnant and due any day. "Other than that, suit yourself."

He closed a tablet on the table in front of him and stood. "If that's all…"

"What about the civilians?" Louise asked.

"Use your discretion," Ryder said flatly. "Except for Williams. She's with me."

Blushing and positive it showed, Sophie quickly added, "To continue to train Phoenix. Right?"

The chief arched a brow and nodded. "Of course. Why else?"

Okay, I am certifiably loopy, Sophie concluded. She made a wry face and turned away. *I may not be coveting the chief and planning to eliminate anybody who got in my way as Carrie has, but my imagination is just as wild.*

Here she'd been, happily entertaining visions of their emotional and perhaps even spiritual connection, when he'd been all business, as usual. His reasons for wanting her around weren't personal, they were merely practical.

She shrugged. Well, one thing about it was good. If Carrie did show up and start killing again, at least Sophie wouldn't end up in the crosshairs.

The subconscious reference to a rifle scope made her frown. Think. Try to clarify an unsettling feeling. *That* was what had been hovering in the back of her mind! Stan had used a pistol when he'd shot her bed. So, where was his rifle?

Lily drove Ryder so crazy about the homecoming celebration and street fair, he let her come to work with him that Friday. The booths didn't open until 10:00 a.m. but he figured she could entertain herself playing with puppies at the training center, if necessary.

That was exactly what she was doing when he went looking for her. Someone, probably Sophie or Gina, had slipped an old shirt on over Lily's good clothes and she was sitting on the floor, laughing, while half-grown pups vied for spots next to her or in her lap.

She beamed up at her daddy. "They love me."

"I can see that. It's almost time for the fair. Tell the dogs goodbye and come with me."

"Okay." It took her several tries to get up amid all the licking and giggling.

"Sorry," Sophie said, hurrying to help. "I lost track of time."

Before Ryder could intercede she scooped up his daughter and carried her inside as he asked, "Are you ready?"

"In a sec. Lily needs her face and hands washed. Did you bring a hairbrush?"

"No. Why?"

"Never mind. It's a girl thing. I'll fix her hair."

The way her mother would, if she had one, Ryder thought, chagrined. Opal Mullins usually took care of readying Lily for school after he dropped her off, so except for church on Sundays, he rarely had to help the little girl primp. Truth to tell, it seldom occurred to him to smooth her tousled, blond hair. He liked the elfin way it made her look.

"Thanks for putting the shirt on her," Ryder said, lingering in the doorway to Sophie's office. "I didn't bring a change of clothes."

"What did you do when she was a baby?"

"I had some help. Her babysitter used to stay with her at my house back then. She took care of laundry and stuff."

Watching while Sophie gently brushed tangles out of the silky blond hair, Ryder remembered to pass on news. "By the way, Tristan won't be on patrol until tomorrow. Ariel just had her baby."

"A girl, right? That's what Ariel said she was expecting."

"I didn't think to ask." He had to smile when Sophie rolled her eyes at him and said, "Men. You never ask the important questions."

"All I know is, the baby is healthy and everybody is doing fine. Tristan is as proud as if he were the natural father."

"I know Ariel wishes he were, but at least her ex can't try to hurt her or the baby anymore. Not ever. I'm glad she has Tristan to lean on. He'll make a great dad."

"And probably remember to bring a hairbrush?"

Sophie laughed. "I wouldn't count on it. He's a man." She presented the purse-size brush to Lily. "Here. You can keep this one. I have others. Let's go."

The child continued to pull the brush through the ends of her hair long after Sophie had finished, as if she were suddenly grown-up. Ryder wasn't sure he liked that.

Another thing he wasn't sure about was spending the entire day with the pretty, head trainer. On a professional level it made perfect sense. On a deeper level it bothered him. A lot. If there was the slightest chance that Carrie was in the vicinity of Desert Valley, his keeping company with any woman was a bad idea.

He supposed he could have asked Gina, the junior trainer, to accompany him but only if he wanted to do battle with rookie Shane Weston to whom she was engaged. Besides, they were a compatible team.

Nor was he willing to endanger another person. Sophie and he already had something of a history, thanks to the criminal actions of her stalker, so why rock the boat?

Ryder huffed and began to smile as he drove toward the town square. Rocking a boat reminded him of sailing which reminded him of *water* which reminded him of—Sophie.

He couldn't even remember the last time he'd had real fun. Felt good enough to actually be playful. Or trusted anyone enough to revert to a former version of himself—a younger, less jaded version. Here he was, nearly thirty, and he had already begun to act like a stuffy old man. Until Sophie had forced her way into his psyche.

Glancing in the rearview mirror, Ryder saw her following in her SUV. She'd asked to transport Phoenix so he'd agreed. It was evident that she'd become attached to the needy dog. He could relate. There was something about the Aussie that brought out similar feelings in him. Plus, Lily loved playing hide-and-seek. Titus wasn't good for more than one or two times but the younger dog usually outlasted his energetic child.

"I want you to stay right with me and the dogs

today," Ryder reminded Lily. "Remember what we talked about. You have to behave so Phoenix and Titus will. It's very important."

She nodded sagely. "I'll be good. I promise. Can I take my brush?"

"Why don't you leave it in the car so you don't lose it? You don't want to disappoint Ms. Sophie."

"She's nice." Grinning, she looked up to her daddy. "You gonna marry her?"

"Whoa! What makes you ask that?"

"I just wondered." Ryder saw her gingerly handling the small brush. "I like her."

"I do, too, honey, but maybe she doesn't want to get married. Some people never do, you know. They prefer to live by themselves."

"Oh."

Satisfied that he'd ended the conversation, Ryder parked on a side street for easy access, then helped Lily out before putting a leash on Titus.

Sophie pulled up behind them with Phoenix. He was dressed in his own bulletproof vest and Ryder hoped the extra level of protection wouldn't make him, or the human officers, too hot as the desert day warmed.

Lily was jumping up and down. "Phoenix is here!"

"That's right," her father said. "Now settle down so you don't get the dogs too excited."

"Okay."

He frowned at Sophie. "Where's your vest?"

"In the car. I'll get it if you insist."

"I insist."

"Okay, but I'm not keeping it fastened tightly."

Ryder was so intent on making Sophie as safe as possible, he failed to see what his daughter was doing until she tugged on the trainer's free hand.

"Ms. Sophie?"

"Yes, Lily?"

"Why don't you want to get married?"

"What makes you think that?"

"Daddy said."

Sophie shot him a cynical glance. "Oh, he did, did he. Well, honey, I'll tell you why. It's because I like living with dogs better than most people."

"Why?"

Ryder hoped her answer was not going to be too serious. When she said, "Because they can't make up stories about me that aren't true," he was relieved. He almost strangled trying to stifle a laugh and was succeeding until she added, "Do you like to play in the water? I know a really funny story about that."

"Too bad you don't take after the dogs more," he interjected. "It would be better if you couldn't talk, either."

Grinning widely, she started off toward the Main Street gathering with Phoenix at her side.

Ryder fell in behind her, one hand in Lily's and the other holding Titus's leash.

"I wanna hear the story, Daddy."

"Maybe later," he said, assuming the child would quickly forget. "We have to see the fair and have some fun first."

And work, Ryder added, holding tight to Lily's hand. He'd almost left her with Opal today but given the positive police reports and Stan Allen's capture, he was relieved enough to let her come along.

After losing his wife, he'd been paranoid about keeping baby Lily isolated. Opal had talked some sense into him in time to keep his fears from permanently scarring his only child. He couldn't keep her to himself forever. He had to let her experience life and just do his best to safeguard her, as any caring parent would.

Besides, Carrie had never seemed affected by the little girl. Her threats and actions had been directed against any adult who had gotten in the way of her romantic fantasies. Lily was probably safer in Desert Valley than anywhere else. Here, everyone not only knew she was the chief's child, they looked out for her as well as each other.

He followed Sophie to the edge of the crowd, paused to radio his position and listened while the other teams checked in. Theoretically, he should be as calm as Titus was acting, yet he was not.

There was something wrong. He could feel it. What he could not do was identify it.

"All set?" Sophie asked lightly.

Ryder nodded. "Yeah. Let's do this."

ELEVEN

Sophie walked a fine line between enjoying herself and working, particularly since Lily kept up a steady stream of chatter, half of which was inherently funny. The child wanted, and got, most of what she begged for.

Lily would tug on Ryder's hand and point, and he would divert to do as she asked. His expression was more than benevolent. It was filled to overflowing with love. Whether she knew it or not, Lily Hayes was a very blessed little girl.

They paused at a booth festooned with paper streamers and filled with gaudy costume jewelry while Lily oohed and aahed.

"Made it all myself," the saleslady said.

Sophie could see tags and markings that indicated otherwise, which was probably why the baubles were so cheap. A sweet child like Lily deserved better. Perhaps, come Christmas, it would be okay for Sophie to buy her something suitable for a little girl. A locket, maybe?

Once, long ago, Sophie recalled having had a golden locket she'd cherished, although where it had come from was buried too deeply to remember. The only clear memory she had of it was the day her mother had been in a foul mood and had ripped it from her neck, saying it was too good for such a naughty girl. The chain had broken. So had Sophie's heart.

It was futile to entertain past hurts, she knew, so she forced a smile. While she'd been daydreaming, Lily had made her selection from the array of plastic jewels and Ryder was paying for her purchase.

"I wanna wear it," Lily shouted above the surrounding din.

When Ryder dropped to one knee in front of his daughter to fasten the clasp of a bright blue-and-green necklace, Sophie was so moved she had to don her sunglasses to hide her eyes. His tenderness was remarkable. More than touching, it was awe inspiring. If more parents were like Ryder, maybe their children would turn out better and the police wouldn't have so much to do.

Contrite almost instantly, Sophie whispered, "Sorry, Father. I know they probably do the best they can." *Like my parents did*, she added. They had an unhappy marriage and sometimes took out frustrations on their only child. That kind of treatment could have left her beaten down, but it had had the opposite effect. It had made her stronger. More independent.

In a strange way, everything in Sophie's life seemed to have directed her choices, to have brought her here at this very time. She did believe that God had a purpose for everyone but had never narrowed it down this way before. That conclusion was enough to refocus her concentration on the milling crowd.

Ryder straightened and touched her arm. "Did you see something?"

"No. I just realized I was daydreaming and decided to pay better attention."

"Good point. I plan to drop Lily at Opal's after we've made a couple of turns around the square."

"Aw, Daddy…"

"I can understand doing that," Sophie agreed. "If she stayed here all day you'd have to take out a loan."

"I want a hot dog."

Sophie laughed. "Just don't let her ride in my car on the way home. I don't recommend the bounce house, either."

"Yeah! I wanna go in there."

"Before lunch, not after," Ryder said, taking her hand and starting toward the ticket seller for the inflatable apparatus.

"You are one soft touch, Chief."

"I know. But Lily and I don't get much chance to do things like this. I'm usually working or she's in school."

"Kindergarten?"

The little girl shook her golden curls. "Uh-uh. First grade. I'm almost six."

"That old?" Sophie couldn't help chuckling along with Ryder when he said, "Six going on sixteen."

"I believe it. I was an only child, too. We tend to mature faster, I think, because we spend so much time talking to adults."

Sophie scanned the crowded street while Ryder escorted his daughter into the play area, then returned.

Lily didn't waste any time getting into the spirit with the other children. She waved at them from behind the black mesh safety net. "Look, Daddy! I can go high!"

"Do you have siblings?" Sophie asked him.

"No. My folks always said they got it right the first time."

"You made that up."

"Actually, no. It was one of Mom's favorite quotes."

"They must not live around here or you'd have her watching Lily while you're at work."

"You're right that they don't live in Arizona. But I'd still use Opal, even if my parents were local."

Sophie's forehead narrowed as she frowned. "Why? Are they inadequate parents like mine were?"

"No." He was shaking his head. "The reason I

favor Opal Mullins is because she used to be an army MP. She knows how to handle herself in a crisis and I figure she's the best person to safeguard Lily." He paused and smiled slightly. "The only drawback is her cats. I can't send Titus with Lily because they don't like dogs."

"I can help with that if Opal will let me. I'd like to see Titus stay with Lily during the day."

"So would I." The radio buzzed. Ryder replied. "Hayes here. What's up?"

All Sophie could catch was a few fragments of words because he was using the earpiece.

"All right. Hold your positions. I'll be right over." His eyes narrowed on the amusement device where Lily was still happily jumping around and bouncing off rubbery supports.

"If you need to go, I'll watch Lily and bring her to you when her time is up." A chill skittered up Sophie's spine. "They didn't sight Carrie, did they?"

"No. Nothing like that. An elderly vendor caught someone shoplifting a pot holder. The buyer is insisting she bought it across the square. She's asking for me because she knows me. If it's who I think it is, she's older than Methuselah. She can wait a few more minutes."

The radio called again. Ryder made a face. "They're actually trying to hit each other now? Okay. I'll hurry." He turned to Sophie. "I won't be long."

"No problem. Which dog do you want to take with you?"

"Probably Titus. He's calmer. Is that okay with you?"

"Sure. Go. I've got this."

She could tell Ryder was hesitant. After he turned and started away he looked back several times. Nevertheless, Sophie was gratified that he trusted her with his daughter.

Shouting from the opposite side of the courthouse was starting to draw an influx of fairgoers. It sounded as if the fight had escalated. Leave it to two elderly women to start a ruckus over a pot holder.

Peering into the bounce house, Sophie didn't see Lily. She started forward. The operator stopped her at the rope fence. "No dogs."

"I just can't see my—my little friend."

"If I put her in there, she's still in there," he insisted. "Now back up, lady."

"This is a police dog," Sophie countered. "Let me through."

"You're no cop."

"No, but the dog is. And I'm with him," she argued.

"I don't care if he's the chief of police. You aren't allowed..." His eyes widened. Leaving her, he sprinted around the apparatus and out of sight.

Trying to figure out why he was agitated, Sophie continued to look through the heavy mesh

156   *Search and Rescue*

for Lily. *There she was! Praise God.* But she had to stoop to see her.

That was what was wrong. The whole contraption was collapsing! Not only was it full of children, it was bound to be suffocating once the air leaked out.

Sophie raced toward the place where she'd seen the entrance. Elastic mesh was hooked to grommets in the thick plastic shell. If she could manage to get one or two of those open she could begin to rescue children.

They were starting to panic and call for their parents by the time she gained access. Adults crowding in behind her took children from her as she lifted them out and passed them back.

Phoenix remained beside her even though she'd had to drop his leash to free both hands. Pressure from above was starting to close the opening as support pillars lost form.

"Lily!" Sophie screamed. "Where are you?"

"Over here." The call was nearly swallowed up by the roar of the frantic crowd and the sound of the air compressor that was supposed to keep the structure full.

"Can you stand up?"

"No," Lily squealed.

"Then crawl to me," Sophie ordered, fighting to keep the exit open with her own shoulders and praying the child could make it before they were both crushed.

"I can't. I'm scared."

"You have to, Lily. I can't hold the door up much longer."

All Sophie heard in reply was weeping. Where was Ryder? Surely he must know he was needed here.

Crowding in beside her, Phoenix put his front paws on the curved edge of the base tube and barked.

"Yes!" Sophie edged aside and used all her strength to push a wider opening. "Go get her. Get Lily."

The dog slipped through the slit between the top and bottom of the structure without hesitation and plunged into the tighter space the way an agility dog would attack a flimsy fabric tunnel.

"Phoenix is coming to get you," Sophie shouted. "Grab his collar and let him bring you out. Lily? Lily, can you hear me?"

Passersby were shouting. Ryder overheard enough to make the hair stand up on the back of his neck. He outran his old dog getting back to Lily.

What he saw when he got closer was a disaster. The heavy rubber frame of the house was barely inflated. Gravity had forced most of the remaining air into the lower portions as the roof and ceiling collapsed. Locals and the operator of the attraction were trying to hold up one edge of the mesh opening while some fool…

His breath caught. That was Sophie. Her legs were kicking.

The reason why the trainer would have put herself in harm's way was immediately evident. Lily must be inside. And, as he listened, he realized a dog was, too.

Ryder flashed his badge and a path cleared in front of him. "What happened?"

"Pump musta failed," the operator said. "We got all the kids out but that crazy woman let her dog in."

"She would only have done that in an emergency," Ryder shouted. "Is there another way in?"

"No. All the other mesh is anchored solid. This is the only part that has a door."

"So far," Ryder said, leaving the others and racing around the four-sided structure. He could see through the rear portion. Lily and Phoenix were hunkered down in a corner that had yet to fully collapse. He couldn't see Sophie from there.

Several slashes with his knife made a hole in the elastic mesh without damaging the inflatable. "Here, Lily. I'm here."

She didn't move even though Ryder enlarged the hole and stuck his arm through. "You have to come to bring me the dog," he said. Nobody would get out of this alive if he had to crawl in and trap himself, too.

The perceived need to help her dog was enough to get Lily moving. She and Phoenix reached the opening together and the dog sailed through in one easy leap.

Ryder grabbed his little girl, pulled her out and held her close. There was no time to rejoice. Not when Sophie was still trapped.

The men who had been supporting the weight to relieve her were perspiring. Their hands kept slipping. He tapped one on the shoulder, said, "You. Help me," then commanded Titus, "Watch," so Lily would be guarded.

Each man grasped one of Sophie's ankles and began to pull. To Ryder's relief, she slid easily and came up dripping with sweat and fighting mad. "No! Let me go. I have to get Lily."

"She's out. She's safe. So is Phoenix," Ryder shouted, fending off her blows. The astonished relief on Sophie's face was more than welcome. It reconfirmed that she was also unhurt, although she was laboring to catch her breath.

As he helped her to her feet and steadied her, she threw her arms around his neck and began to sob. Ryder let her. He could feel tears of joy in his own eyes. Not only was his darling Lily safe and sound, this brave woman had risked her own life for her.

Overcome by the reality of what had just happened, he held Sophie close and stroked her back without hesitation. He didn't care if the whole

town saw him and the rumors started to fly. No
amount of thanks or hugs would repay this debt.
He owed her everything.

At his side he felt the tug of a small hand.
"Daddy?"

His arms opened. He bent down and scooped
up the child he could have lost only moments before.

Sophie backed off barely enough to allow room
for Lily, then wrapped an arm around her, too, and
showered her with kisses.

Ryder did the same. He even made a few errors
and kissed Sophie's damp hair. When he thought
about what could easily have happened, it chilled
him to the bone.

"Hey!" the attraction's operator yelled. "You
owe me for a ruined net."

Ryder ignored him until he added. "It wasn't
my fault the thing collapsed. Somebody messed
with my air pump!"

"Can you stand?" Ryder asked Sophie.

Sniffling and wiping her cheeks, she nodded.

"Then take care of Lily again. I'm leaving both
dogs with you."

He used his radio to summon the rookies on
duty and circled the apparatus. Parts of the large
compressor looked dented but it seemed to be running okay.

Ryder put Shane in charge of setting up a
perimeter and told James Harrison to use Hawk's

bloodhound's nose to scout for evidence. Ellen Foxcroft and Carly, her golden retriever, tried to strike a trail but there had been too many people milling around for the dog to work well.

"Probably vandals," the operator remarked. "Kids love to hang around back here. I saw more of 'em today. It's not the first time they've fooled with my equipment. But it is the first time it's gone down so fast. I usually have plenty of time to evacuate. You should see my insurance premiums."

"Here," James called. "Look at this damage, Chief."

The operator stuck his head in to look, too. "You cops must've done that when you cut the mesh."

Ryder didn't bother arguing. He knew better. He might not have a clue who had stabbed the base of the inflated house but he knew it hadn't been him. If he ever got his hands on the kids who had thought it would be fun to bring down the attraction, he was going to lock them up long enough to make an impression they'd never forget.

He scanned the crowd, looking for guilty expressions. The only ones who seemed upset were the parents of the other children Sophie had saved. If the town didn't give her a medal for what she did, he might see about getting her one himself.

Returning to her and Lily, he saw that someone

had given them bottled water. He smiled and patted Phoenix. "Good boy."

"I never taught him that," Sophie said proudly. "I suppose he could have picked it up by watching me training other dogs but it may have been instinctive. Either way, I was surprised when he followed my commands to get Lily."

"We play that game at home," Ryder told her. "I'm glad you sent him to live with us before today."

"Me, too."

"I want to thank you. For everything," Ryder said quietly. His vision blurred. "I could have lost Lily." *Or both of you.*

Sophie coughed and chuckled at the same time. "In case this ever comes up again, please keep in mind that I *hate* closed spaces."

"Noted. I hope it wasn't that far down when you crawled in."

"No. I saw it going and started to pull kids out." Her eyes widened. "I got them all, didn't I?"

"Yes. Lily was the last."

"You're sure?" Shivering, she glanced toward the police line. "If there's anybody still..."

"I'm sure. They took a head count as they went in and we've talked to the parents. The kids are all accounted for."

"Thank the Lord."

"I already did. And I thanked Him for you, too, Sophie. What you did was above and beyond. It took quick thinking and decisiveness. Most people stood there and screamed but nobody else acted."

She coughed again and grinned at him. "Just remember that the next time you accidentally get wet in the training center bath area."

It was impossible for Ryder to keep from smiling back at her. "After today, I might actually let you get away with it again."

"Often?" she quipped.

"Once," he said, faking a scowl. "You weren't amazing enough for twice." But she was, he reasoned. His heart swelled with the thought of her selflessness and he yearned to pull her and Lily back into his arms again.

Closing his eyes he thought, *Lord help me. And continue to protect those I love.*

The simple prayer shook him to the core. He couldn't argue, though. What he could do was continue to keep his distance and pray somebody took Carrie Dunleavy into custody soon.

He looked out over the crowd. Most of the fairgoers had resumed their meandering and stopped paying much attention to the deflated bounce house now that the excitement was over.

They didn't even seem to care that their chief of police had stood in the street embracing his daughter's pretty rescuer. Teasing from his own officers would come later, of course. That was a given. It wasn't them he was worried about.

Surely, if Carrie had returned to a town where

she'd lived for years, somebody would have noticed her. There had been plenty about her crimes reported in the newspapers, both locally and statewide.

Except that she was the kind of person who was so plain, so unremarkable, she was practically invisible. For all he knew, dozens had stared right at her and paid no attention, especially if she'd made any effort at disguise.

Like it or not, in the mob they had in Desert Valley for this homecoming and fair, almost anybody who tried to move around undetected would succeed.

TWELVE

Sophie wasn't a bit surprised when Ryder took Lily to her babysitter's early. Between the radiating heat and the excitement, both good and bad, they were all wrung out.

She ducked under the colorful canvas canopy of a booth where a friend from church was selling cookbooks. "Whew! Shade."

"Here, have a seat. I need to stretch my legs."

Sophie gladly collapsed into the folding chair. "Thanks, Hazel. It's sure a scorcher."

The elderly woman laughed and patted her own brow with a tissue. "Honey, it's always hot here. I'd move up to Flagstaff in a flash if it wasn't for my aching bones."

"I guess there are advantages," Sophie agreed. "And it does cool off at night pretty well."

"Want more water, dear? I've got a cooler full."

"In a minute. First, Phoenix needs a drink." She bent over, gave the proper command and slowly

poured water from her own bottle into her palm
so he could lap it up.

"Smart pup you got there. I see he's one of
them police dogs. It always surprises me that they
don't all look like Rin Tin Tin. You know, German shepherds."

"A lot of war dogs are," Sophie explained. "We
like to use a variety of breeds for their special-
ized skills. I never turn down a dog that shows
promise."

"What about them other dogs, the ones that help
folks? You know, Ms. Ellen's."

"Companion dogs? For the most part they have
a different temperament. They're more owner ori-
ented and less outwardly concerned. It's hard to
get a dog to open a door for you if he's more interested in barking at what may be on the other side."

"True." While Sophie relaxed and momentarily
closed her eyes, Hazel turned away to wait on a
customer for a cookbook. When she finished she
asked, "What's wrong with him?"

Sophie straightened. Tensed. "Who?"

"Your dog. See?"

Phoenix pressed against her calf and stood as
rigidly as a show dog in the judging ring. His ears
perked, his body quivered.

Following his line of sight, Sophie saw nothing
unusual. But clearly the dog did. Was he picking
up vibes of danger or sensing something familiar?
If she had worked with him longer she'd have had

a better idea. Since his specialty was search and rescue, she wondered if Ryder was back. That was a possibility. So was the idea that another rookie officer and dog had come closer. Most of the animals got along pretty well with the exception of the ones trained for attack and apprehension. By necessity they had to have an edgy temperament.

Phoenix growled.

Sophie rose slowly, deliberately and stepped away from her friend, just in case.

"What's got his hackles up?" Hazel asked.

"Beats me. I'm going to walk around a bit. Thanks for sharing your shade."

"Anytime."

It would have pleased Sophie greatly to have spotted Ryder in the crowd. Not only was his presence comforting, he had their radio. Without him, she was cut off unless she chose to use her cell phone.

"What a great idea." She whipped it out and paged down to his name and number.

"Hayes."

"Where are you?" Sophie asked.

"Just coming up on the square. Is there a problem?"

Frowning, she continued to search for familiar faces. "I'm not sure. Phoenix alerted and I can't figure out why. I thought he might have seen you."

"Hang on," Ryder said. She heard him contacting the other officers by radio before he came back to her. "Might be he scented Ellen and Carly," he said. "They're over by the Friends of the Library used book sales booth. Why don't you join them? I'll be there in a few minutes."

"Okay. Thanks."

"Sophie?"

Waiting for him to continue speaking, she noticed that she had begun to feel as jittery as the dog was acting. "Yes?"

"Be careful."

"I am. It's just hard to see trouble coming when there are so many happy people all around me." *But better than having to go down a dark alley like the night Wes was shot*, she added to herself.

"You keep telling me that dog is as good as Titus. If you really think so, you need to trust him."

"I do. I'm on my way to the library booth. See you there." She ended the call and stepped out.

Phoenix kept pace, his side brushing her calf. He looked every inch a police dog on duty. Even if he had not been wearing his ID halter and vest he would have been formidable. With them, he was magnificent.

And extremely tense, she added, keeping a lookout. The formerly frightened animal had transformed into the working police dog she had envisioned when she'd first seen him. Even better, he was intuitive beyond measure.

So, what was he sensing? What familiar odor

was he picking up that had put him on high alert? She had never introduced him to anything taken from Carrie's desk or her home, so it couldn't be that. Unless…

Sophie almost broke and ran for cover when she made a leap of reasoning. Phoenix had been with Lily in the bounce house and had exited near where the vandal had stood when he or she had slashed into it. Was he clever enough to have remembered that scent and recognized it again? It was normal for him to recall people he knew. Strangers were another matter.

She spotted Ellen and waved as she quickened her pace. Carly wasn't acting strange, yet Phoenix was. What did that mean?

They met beneath a bunch of balloons tacked to an upright board above the awning. "Boy, am I glad to see you're okay," Ellen told her.

"Yeah. You, too. Has your dog been nervous?"

"Not that I've noticed." The rookie officer eyed Sophie. "Maybe Phoenix is mirroring your mood. You're still keyed up."

That brought a sigh. "I suppose I am. I was afraid I was going to run out of air in that stinky prison of rubber and plastic."

"But you saved a bunch of scared kids."

"By the grace of God." She kept searching the gathering. "Have you heard any more from the chief?"

"Not since a couple of minutes ago when he told us to keep an eye out for you," Ellen said.

"Radio and tell him I'm okay, will you, while I try to figure out what's wrong with this dog."

"Whatever it is, it seems to be catching," the rookie said. "Look at Carly."

Both dogs were now erect, alert and facing the same direction.

"I thought Phoenix might be reacting to the scent of whoever sabotaged the bounce house but Carly wouldn't be, would she?"

"She might. We took part in that search."

Sophie rested her palm on the butt of her gun, leaving it secure in the holster on her hip.

Ryder appeared in the distance with Titus at his side, bringing joy to her heart and calm to her nerves. She began to smile. Her partner was back. Their working relationship might be temporary but at least it would last for the weekend.

A bang sounded. The professionals ducked while most fairgoers merely looked around, confused.

One of the balloons arrayed above the booth had burst. Sophie was about to laugh at herself for being afraid when a second one exploded.

She shouted, "Shots fired. Everybody down!"

From Ryder's viewpoint the scene was chaos. All he could do was clear that portion of the street.

It took several tries to convince revelers to take cover but he was finally satisfied.

A radio call assembled his staff. "Williams and Foxcroft say the shots hit that board up there with the balloons. Harrison, take it down and check for bullets. If you find anything, bag it and save it for the state crime lab."

"Yes, sir. Did you get your daughter out of here okay?"

Ryder nodded. "She's at Opal's." His gaze drifted to Sophie again. After the arrest of Stan Allen he'd thought she'd be safe. Now he was not so sure.

These shots had been even farther afield than the ones at the depot had. Still, if that was due to poor targeting, why had balloons burst every time? This shooter seemed to be aiming all right, just not at people. *Or at Sophie*, he concluded with relief. That had to be a good sign.

He approached her as soon as he'd put the others to work. "I think you should call it a day."

"Why?"

"Because you're not a cop anymore."

"As you keep reminding me," she countered, making a face. "It was my dog who alerted first."

Frowning, he studied the Aussie. "Really? Why would he?"

"I haven't figured that out yet. I thought it might be because he smelled the perp who slashed the bounce house but that seems a little far-fetched."

"Yes, it does. We never put him on that trail."

"Right. But Ellen had Carly tracking and she did perk up after we joined them. I suggest you and I stick together and let the dog go where he wants. He might strike a trail again."

"You're determined to stay here no matter what, aren't you?" When a smile lit Sophie's face and made her hazel eyes sparkle, he was positive.

"Well…"

"All right. But if one more thing happens, if you even sneeze, you're done. Understood?"

"Yes, *sir*."

"And don't you dare salute me," he warned. "We've already provided enough material to keep the gossip mill running for months."

"Hey, it wasn't my fault I got stuck in the collapse and had to be yanked out."

Against his better judgment he slipped an arm around her waist and briefly pulled her closer. "No, but it was my fault I hugged you. I was so grateful I couldn't help myself. I still am."

"No problem," she quipped. "The next time I feel a good cry coming on I'll know whose shoulder to choose."

"Anytime," Ryder said.

"You mean that, don't you?"

"Absolutely." His gaze switched from her to the distance, where his men were taking down the board with the balloons. Once again, he could have lost her.

The notion of spending the rest of his life without Sophie in it was unacceptable. Even if they never progressed past being good friends, he wanted her around.

Now, all he had to do was see to it that nobody robbed him of the *second* woman he had ever loved.

As far as Sophie was concerned, it didn't matter where the dog led them as long as Ryder stayed beside her. She was less frightened than angry. This wasn't the last straw but it was getting close. There was only so much harassment one person could take. Of course, Stan's attacks had been serious threats. But those were over now that he was in jail. The notion that he may have had accomplices had been refuted. He'd grieved his brother alone and his attempts at retribution had been committed solo. They were sure of that because he had proudly admitted to stalking Sophie and invading her home.

One unsettling thought made her touch Ryder's arm. "Stan didn't get out on bail, did he?"

"Not a chance. Besides, he hasn't been arraigned yet."

"Oh. I just thought maybe…"

"Pinning today's problems on him would be nice. Trouble is, he can't have done it." Ryder was shaking his head thoughtfully.

"Is it possible that the incident today involving Lily is connected in some way?" Sophie asked.

"We can't rule it out. It's normal to imagine conspiracies everywhere when we've experienced them before. Try not to let it get you down."

"Okay. I just wish we'd heard something about Carrie lately. The business with Stan was unfortunate because it distracted us."

Looking somber, Ryder nodded. "Anything that threatens you is distracting. That doesn't mean I can't do my job."

"I didn't mean that." She made a face. "Well, maybe I did, just a little. There's only so much your police department can do, even with the extra officers Marian is funding."

Again, he gave her a grim look. "Yes. And Ellen says her mother is starting to show real improvement. Doctors expect her to come out of the coma very soon."

"That's wonderful! I hated to keep asking poor Ellen about it and make her keep telling me how bad Marian is doing."

"I know what you mean."

"So, what do you think will happen when Marian recovers? It's been months since she agreed to pay for all the rookies to stay to solve the murders. If she'd been conscious when Carrie's crimes were discovered, do you think she'd have withdrawn her support?"

"I don't know. It doesn't matter right now." Ryder paused at a street corner, deciding which way to proceed. Neither dog seemed inclined to patrol further. He shaded his eyes with one hand beside the brim of his cap. "Which way?"

Sophie shrugged. "Beats me. The four-legged officers seem to be ready for a drink of water and a nap in the shade."

"That makes three of us."

"Four," Sophie said. "I think my adrenaline is wearing off. I'm practically asleep on my feet."

"Which is why you should go home. Take a couple hours' break, then come back if you want to."

"I could freshen up, too," she added, glancing at her damp clothing and feeling the effects of perspiration.

Ryder gave her a lopsided smile. "Now *there's* a good idea."

"What? You don't appreciate the perfume of old plastic and sweaty kids? Imagine that."

"You could just go bathe the dogs again. I've heard that can be refreshing."

"Oh, have you?" The urge to apologize again for dousing him was strong. She squelched it. After all, he was the one who had brought it up this time and was acting as if he'd forgiven her. So why destroy the mood of camaraderie by being contrite, particularly since she didn't feel all that repentant any more.

"It would be simpler to use the facilities at the training center instead of going all the way home," Sophie said. "Is there a guard posted today?"

"Just Benny. He's stayed more alert since he was attacked a while back but he's not a young man."

"It still helps to have somebody there." She checked the street that led to where she'd parked her official SUV. "Walk me to my car?"

Ryder fell in beside her with Titus. "This poor old guy is really tired. Why don't you take him back with you and kennel him? I'll continue to work Phoenix. Maybe he'll alert again and I can figure out what upset him."

"Fair enough." Smiling, Sophie swapped the ends of the dogs' leashes and the K-9s switched places as smoothly as if they had recently practiced.

"I need to run more refresher courses soon," Sophie said as they strolled toward her parked vehicle. "These rookies need it and I have a long list of queries asking for retraining."

"Dogs or handlers?"

"Both." Sighing, she stopped beside her SUV. "What's going to be tough is making sure any department where they go is still in the market for a team, both K-9 and handler. Keeping these rookies here in Desert Valley for six months may have messed up their former plans."

"I'd thought of that. I'd never let myself be separated from Titus no matter what."

Sophie smiled. "That won't happen once he's retired and becomes your pet. I know how hard it is to let go of a wonderful companion and great student like Phoenix. Even though you'll be keeping him in town I miss having him at home with me."

At the mention of his name, the dog's ears pricked.

"Yes, you," she responded quietly. Breaking one of her own cardinal rules she patted his head while he was supposed to be working, then loaded Titus and bid Ryder goodbye.

The sight of the chief, standing tall with Phoenix at his side, almost choked her up. It didn't matter how many times she told herself that she was merely the dog's trainer, she felt a swelling of pride every time she was able to pair a great dog with a deserving officer.

The same went for Ellen's service dog project. Although the commands differed, the animal's willingness to listen was just as vital to success. All in all, Sophie had to repeatedly thank God for putting her in this place at this time and letting her do the work for which she was best suited.

Feeling gratitude, she drove toward the training center. If it weren't for criminals she'd be out of a job. Nevertheless, it would be awfully nice to have a respite from being shot at. That thought made her smile. Chances were that once Carrie Dunleavy was captured they'd all begin complaining about life being too dull!

Right now, however, when she was bone weary

and in desperate need of a shower and clean clothes, not to mention a chance to wash her hair, Sophie was ready for a little R & R.

Habit made her check her rearview mirror. There was nobody there who looked dangerous. No black car with dark windows like the one that had been abandoned in the street when she'd cracked her head. No long, evening shadows that might hide rattlesnakes.

She should have been able to take a deep breath, relax and chill out. Should have. But couldn't. Evident threats were not the worst kind.

It was the enemy who remained unseen that always proved the deadliest.

THIRTEEN

Now that the two most important people and one dog in his life were away from the street fair, Ryder was better able to concentrate. He'd argued with himself constantly that his capabilities were not affected by the presence of others, but the facts spoke for themselves.

Well, at least he wasn't ignoring the special ones in favor of focusing only on his job the way he used to. Yes, it was necessary to prioritize. But it wasn't always possible to separate earthly responsibility from God-given duty. Take Shane and Gina, for instance. He'd paired them for a reason. They were good together and, if parted, might worry about each other too much.

His pastor had recently preached that worry was a sin because it showed a lack of faith and trust in divine providence. Perhaps. Probably. Unfortunately, it was also a human trait and he was very human.

Human enough to fall in love again? Ryder

asked himself. Maybe. Although it was also possible that forced proximity was affecting him, making him believe that what he felt for Sophie was love when it was actually deep concern.

All that was sensible. And logical. So why did his pulse start to speed when he saw her and why did his spirits lift when she smiled? Moreover, why did he feel devastated when he thought he might lose her?

His cell phone buzzed. "Hayes."

"We've had a possible sighting of the boys who slashed the blow-up house," Tristan said. "I didn't want to use the radio and take a chance of being overheard."

"Where?"

"East end of the square, near where it's piled up," he reported. "I guess they're admiring their handiwork."

"Copy. On my way. Keep them in sight but don't apprehend until I get there."

"Affirmative."

Wending his way through the thinning crowd, Ryder kept an eye on Phoenix, looking for a reaction. He got a strong one as soon as he stepped off the curb next to the collapsed attraction. The Aussie bristled, his hair sticking up between the straps of his vest.

As soon as the dog stopped, one front foot in the air like a bird dog, Ryder saw the teens, too.

They stopped laughing and jostling each other

when one of them spotted the dog and pointed. All four boys exchanged glances. Ryder wasn't close enough to hear what they were saying to each other but their body language was clear.

He keyed his mic. "Move in. It's them."

The teens scattered as if they were a flock of wild birds and he was a circling hawk. He was glad Phoenix wasn't trained for apprehension because he wanted to bring these hoodlums down himself.

One jumped over a stroller, narrowly missing the baby in it, and sped off down the sidewalk, right into Tristan McKeller's arms. His yellow Lab, Jesse, helped and Tristan had him in custody immediately.

The second and third suspects went left together. Shane and German shepherd Bella made short work of them.

That left a blond one for Ryder and Phoenix. The dog was almost as determined as his human partner. Zigzagging through a gathering of old-timers, sitting in lawn chairs and reminiscing, Phoenix followed the fleeing vandal step for step. Ryder released him and cut around to where he thought the kid would end up.

He was right. And almost too late. Ryder tackled the teen around the legs. Phoenix leaped on top of them both, barking and growling.

By the time the chief was back on his feet and had his prisoner ready to be handcuffed, the kid was crying like a baby. "I didn't do nothin'. It was all Sammy and Brad's idea. Honest."

"You got drugs on you?" Ryder asked.

"No, I swear."

"Prove it."

Reacting without thinking it through, the boy reached into the pockets of his jeans and came up with a handful of change, dollar bills—and a pocketknife.

Ryder smiled. "You're under arrest." Cuffing him he started to lead him away. "Since you're a minor, I imagine you'll want to call your parents."

"Hey, we was just foolin' around. You know. Kids can't be held for real crimes. They said."

He spun the youth and grabbed him by the shoulders to bring them face-to-face. "*Who* said?"

"Nobody, man, nobody. I was just tellin' you. You know?"

"What I know is that you and your buddies almost killed a bunch of little kids. That's assault, at the very least. About fifteen separate counts of it. And if I find out that somebody paid you to vandalize the ride, it'll be even worse."

"Hey, it was an accident. We didn't know it would go down so fast, man. Why are you so mad?"

"Because one of those kids was my daughter," Ryder said, reminding himself to behave professionally when what he wanted to do was turn this would-be thug over his knee then and there. Granted, he hadn't been a perfect citizen while growing up but he'd never endangered any lives. And he'd certainly never have done someone else's dirty work for any amount of money. That was the difference.

When he recalled the sight of Sophie, stuck half in and half out of the weighty apparatus, it made his blood boil. And the image of Lily, trapped inside, would be with him for the rest of his life. He knew that as surely as he knew his own name.

Anger is unproductive, Ryder kept insisting. Nevertheless, he was still riled when he turned his prisoner over to Shane, Tristan and the others.

"The booths will be closing soon and there shouldn't be any foot traffic until tonight when they have the hometown concert and street dance. I'll transport these prisoners to the lockup while the rest of you finish here. We'll regroup at the station at seven."

Nodding to James he added, "Since your girlfriend, Madison, is still hanging around looking for news for the *Gazette*, you can be the last to leave."

James Harrison nodded. "What about the booths for overnight? Most of the vendors are leaving their stuff right here."

"They say they have their own after-hours patrol," Ryder answered. "Personally, that suits me fine. Has anybody seen Sophie since I sent her to the training center to put Titus up and take a break?"

Each, in turn, answered in the negative. Ryder wasn't too worried. After all, they had Stan in custody and now the idiotic vandals were also out of commission. That left only Carrie Dunleavy and no matter how many old-timers and other locals he had asked, nobody had seen hide nor hair of her.

"Tell you what. Tristan, you're probably more than ready to go visit Ariel and that new baby. You take our prisoners to the station and I'll go to the training center. When you've locked them up you can go. I'll take care of the paperwork when I get there later."

"Yes, sir. Thanks. My sister, Mia, has been staying with Ariel but I need to check for myself."

"Understood."

Ryder certainly did understand. Although he had not ordered Sophie to come back to the square by a certain time, he'd expected her by now. Or sooner. She was the kind of person who always wanted to be in the thick of things.

He headed for his car with Phoenix at his side, not running but not dawdling, either. With each step his anxiety built.

By the time he was on the road back to the station, all he could think of was making sure that Sophie was all right. It would have helped if scenarios of danger and harm had not kept popping into his fertile mind.

If the following day of the street fair was half as troubling as this first day had been, he was going to need a long rest afterward. Preferably one that did not include nightmares of the former police department secretary. Carrie had been so clever, so unassuming, so good an actress, that everyone, Chief Earl Jones included, had never suspected her evil, manipulative side.

Chances were, that was the characteristic which would eventually bring her downfall. She'd wanted him enough to kill to get him. When that plan had failed she'd transferred her fatal fantasies to two other blond officers, murdering them in turn when they'd cluelessly ignored her. There had not been anything Carrie wouldn't try in the past. Her makeshift shrine to unrequited love had demonstrated that.

Nothing had changed. She might not be here yet but she would be. It was a given. And when she reappeared, Ryder and his officers were going to catch her.

They had to.

Sophie had showered and changed into the clean clothes she'd left in her locker at the training center. The cargo shorts and faded T-shirt were fine for kennel work but not up to the standards she felt would properly represent the K-9 Unit, so she didn't go back to the fair. Instead, she busied herself by cleaning pens, exercising pups by letting them play in the fenced yard and getting the evening meal ready for all her furry charges.

"This stuff actually smells good," she told the two German shepherds and three golden retrievers vying for position at her feet. "I must be really hungry."

Their response to her light conversational tone was to wiggle and jump and pant as if she were about to present them with the tastiest meal they'd ever enjoyed.

Sophie glanced at the wall clock. "It's half an hour early but I guess you guys can eat." Holding stainless steel bowls high she led the way to their nighttime quarters and edged the gate open with her foot. "Okay. Everybody in."

The eager pups not only entered, they sat for her. Well, almost. Their hind legs were bent but their rears were barely planted. "Is that the best *sit* you can do?" she asked, emphasizing the command.

Coming close and holding the position for a few seconds was good enough for dogs this young and excitable. Sophie was quick with the food reward and command to eat so they wouldn't lose control.

She was grinning as she closed and latched the door to their kennels. Puppies were always fed first because they had such a hard time settling down if they thought they might miss a meal.

A metal door clanked somewhere in the building. At least she thought it did. With so much barking and yipping around her she wasn't sure.

"This roof could collapse and I probably wouldn't hear it," she mused, still smiling. Many of the runs for older working dogs were empty because those K-9s were still out with their handlers. She fed some half-grown dogs she was testing for suitability, then went back for more food.

"It's just you and me, Titus," she told the old Lab as she passed his run. "So, what shall we have for supper? I'd like a steak, myself."

His otter-like tail thumped on the floor. Now that she was finished with the more rambunctious dogs, she opened his gate and let him walk with her into the kitchen area. "What does the chief feed you at home? I imagine it's not all kibble. You are probably spoiled rotten."

Panting so that his mouth resembled a smile, he gazed up at her and wagged his tail. "Uh-huh. I thought so. I'll give you a few treats to tide you over until your handler gets here. I'm sure he has something wonderful at home to eat." She thumped his broad back with the flat of her hand. "You don't look as if you've missed many meals."

"Woof."

"Exactly," Sophie joked, behaving as if he were agreeing with her. "The chief is a good guy. You should be thankful you ended up with him."

And so am I, Sophie thought.

She was scratching the mild-mannered yellow Lab's ears when he suddenly stopped panting. The fur at his ruff stood up, making him appear lion-like.

Sophie wished she'd closed the door from the runs because the constant noise was drowning out less prominent sounds. She stood still and strained to listen.

"I don't hear anything, Titus," she whispered. "Are you sure?"

A growl rumbled. What she couldn't hear, she felt as a vibration beneath her touch on his back.

"Okay. I believe you." Reaching for her holstered gun she realized she had taken the belt off when she'd showered and changed. That meant it was still upstairs in the break room, the apartment that had once belonged to her predecessor, another of Carrie's victims.

Thoughts of Carrie were enough to get Sophie moving. "Titus, heel," she whispered, knowing the well-seasoned dog would obey without fail.

Keeping her back to the walls as much as possible, Sophie inched into the office space, then down a short hallway to the stairs leading to the unoccupied apartment. Even if that was where the bothersome noises had originated, she needed to reach her gun. Laying it aside was a rookie move, one Sophie was not proud of.

Each step brought her closer to her goal. She would have donned the uncomfortable bulletproof vest if it had not also been discarded with her dirty clothes.

Titus paced her most of the way, then stepped ahead at the last moment. Sophie reached to stop him and missed his collar.

The sound of a slamming door came from below. The dog hesitated. Cocked his head to listen. Then he left her, turned and galloped back down the stairs.

Sophie didn't know what to do. If there was a menace in the break room she needed to see about it. If Ryder or one of the other K-9 officers had just come in, however, it would be foolish to investigate by herself.

That would mean she'd have to admit to leaving her sidearm unattended, she realized. But this was not the time for pride over prudence. Wheeling, she followed Titus.

Ryder dropped Phoenix's leash and let him drag it while he greeted his faithful old Lab. When he looked up and spotted Sophie he didn't know whether to hug her or chastise her.

"Where have you been?"

"Here. Why?"

"I've been trying to call your cell for the last hour."

"Ah, well, that's a long story. When I came back to change, I took off my holster and vest and left them with the phone. I was just about to go up-stairs to get them."

"Well, go." He could tell by the way she was shifting from one foot to the other that something else was up. "What's wrong?"

"Titus acted as if he'd heard somebody up there. We were about to see when you came and he forgot about everything else."

"It's not like him to abandon a search."

"He wasn't wearing his working harness so he probably figured it wasn't important. That, or he really is losing his edge."

"Maybe a little of both," Ryder said. He drew his gun. "You stay down here with the dogs. I'll go check it out."

"I left my stuff on the little table by the bath-room door," Sophie said. "Sorry."

"You're not supposed to have to defend your-self in here. Where's Benny Sims?"

"It's still too early for him to be on guard duty."

There had been a time when they hadn't felt the need for any extra protection, Ryder remembered with chagrin. Those were the days.

As he started for the stairway, he was totally alert. Each step was calculated, controlled. Using a two-handed approach he whipped around the corner into the upper rooms.

They were deserted. There was a lingering scent of flowery shampoo, undoubtedly a result of Sophie's earlier presence, but no prowler. No menace. Nothing out of place except the equipment she had left behind.

Ryder holstered his gun and picked up hers, handling it carefully. He was turning to go back down when he heard Titus and Phoenix begin to bark.

Sophie screamed.

A door slammed. Echoed.

Ryder sailed downstairs, his boots barely touching the wooden steps.

"Sophie!"

FOURTEEN

She flew straight to Ryder as soon as he reappeared in the stairwell. Though he did slip one arm around her waist he kept his gun hand clear. "What happened?"

"I don't know." It was embarrassing to have screeched like a dog that had tried to eat a beehive, but her nerves had been so on edge lately she was glad that was *all* she'd done. "You went upstairs, then the dogs started to bark and something crashed into me."

"Did you get a look at whatever it was?"

"No. As soon as I hit the floor my so-called bodyguards were all over me."

"I should have left Phoenix in harness. Titus is the one who really surprises me. I thought he had more sense."

"Dogs can get senile. We don't usually notice it because they don't talk, but they may forget things."

"Like chasing the bad guys instead of licking the victims?"

Sophie huffed. "Yeah. Something like that. I suppose, if they were really worried about me, they'd have given chase."

"Not if they knew the prowler."

"Carrie?" She could hardly make herself say it.

"Or one of the volunteers or cadets who help out. It could also have been a stranger, somebody who knew we'd all be busy at the street fair and thought it was a good time for a raid."

"Here? What were they after, kibble?"

"Or vests or ammo or even the dogs. You never know with crooks."

"True. It seems to me that if Carrie were involved she wouldn't have run off. She'd have confronted me or tried to hurt me."

"Logically, yes. Stay here. I'm going to go check the entire building."

Left with the dogs and rearmed for self-defense, she kept both of them leashed and close. Nevertheless, she was filled with relief when Ryder returned.

"Nothing?"

"Nothing. I'd already done a walk-through upstairs when you yelled. There was nothing wrong up there, either."

"Okay. We'll chalk it up to my nerves. Now that I think about it, it may have been Phoenix who bumped into me from behind and sent me flying."

"What changed your mind?"

"The fact that they didn't try to chase anybody.

All they were interested in was licking me. Maybe they felt guilty."

"Or maybe you tasted good. Did you have a corn dog at the fair?"

"Hours ago. Titus and I were talking about getting a steak for supper before he alerted to the upstairs rooms. He thought steak was a great idea." The smile she had expected bloomed on Ryder's face.

"He would."

"Of course," Sophie quipped, "he's very smart." She lowered her voice as if the dog might actually understand what she was about to say. "At least he used to be. I'm so glad you've agreed to retire him."

"Not so fast," Ryder countered. "He can still take part in things like stakeouts and help with tracking. All we have to do is make it easy on him."

"Speaking of which," she added, "what do you propose to do about Eddie, Dennis and Louise. Eddie's a little younger than the others but they're all vested so they can safely retire at any time."

"And make room for a few of the rookies who might want to stay on once Carrie is caught and we can officially tie her to Veronica's murder and the attack on Marian Foxcroft? I'd thought of that." He glanced at her. "So, how about that steak dinner? Minus the dogs. The Canyon Steakhouse serves a good rib eye."

Sophie blushed and made a face. "I can't go to a nice restaurant when I'm dressed like a refugee from a hobo jungle."

"You're not *that* bad." Ryder was chuckling.

"Thanks a heap, Chief."

"You're welcome. As soon as some of the others drift back to the station, I'll have a couple of them dust doors and the upstairs for strange fingerprints. Until then, you have time to go home and change."

Her eyes narrowed and she peered at him. "This is starting to sound suspiciously like a date. And I don't think that's a very good idea."

Laughing, he shook his head. "You have quite an imagination, Ms. Williams. Tell you what. I'll order a couple of large pizzas delivered to the station and you can come join us over there if you want to. Is that impersonal enough to suit you?"

"It's better, even if I won't get my steak," she said, hoping she was successfully concealing her disappointment. Everything she'd said was true. They should not give anybody ideas about them dating, yet she couldn't help wishing he'd have argued with her about dinner, at least a little. He didn't seem to have trouble disagreeing about pretty much everything else.

As for the notion of a prowler, Sophie was beginning to realize that Ryder had been placating her.

He obviously believed she had imagined a

threat this time—and maybe he was right. The whole town had been on edge for months, not to mention the heightened awareness once Carrie's crimes were identified and made public.

After the harrowing day she'd had, Sophie figured her own nerves had to be as overstimulated as those of a puppy chasing a favorite toy. She was a thinking, reasonable human being who needed to settle down and stop letting her imagination carry her away. If she kept calling for help when there was no need, Ryder and the others would soon stop racing to her rescue.

Oh, they'd respond. It was their duty. But they might not hurry enough to keep a real threat from ending her life. And she wasn't finished living. Not by a long shot.

Ryder kept his promise. He and Shane had time to discuss the day's events while rookies James Harrison and Whitney Godwin went with Officer Harmon to fingerprint the training building.

"You told everybody to use the side doors?" Ryder asked.

Shane nodded. "And to stay downstairs. Do you think they'll find any usable prints?"

"This time? No." Ryder shook his head.

"Then what scared Sophie?"

He shrugged. "I have no idea. The stress on all of us has been bad. It's possible she has the kind of mind that invents trouble."

"You don't really believe that, do you?"

Sighing, Ryder said, "Beats me. She hasn't acted like herself since the depot shooting. Trouble has followed her like a lonely pup."

"She was a cop once. Maybe she misses the excitement and is seeing danger everywhere."

"Possibly. But that doesn't explain everything."

"You mean since we arrested her late partner's crazy brother? Before that, the attacks come back to him. Right?"

Ryder's brow knit and he slowly shook his head. "I wonder. Do they? He hasn't admitted to anything besides making threats and breaking into Sophie's house. That leaves all the rifle attacks unexplained."

"So, he had two guns. He probably stashed the rifle after missing so often."

"What about today? In the square? Somebody else shot at those balloons right over her head."

"Somebody whose aim is a whole lot better," Shane reminded him. "If the shooter had wanted to hit one of us, he could have."

"I suppose so. I'll be anxious to get the ballistics report back. If we find out that the bullets at the depot match the ones fired at the training center and the fair, we'll have to rethink the whole scenario."

"You still think it's Carrie?"

"No. The MO doesn't fit her. She likes to be face-to-face."

Ryder could tell that the rookie was struggling. "Go ahead. Spit it out. Say what you're thinking."

"Okay. You asked for it." Shane cleared his throat. "Think all the way back. Her first victim was shot, perhaps from a distance. Then one was pushed down the stairs. That was a hands-on crime. But the next was arson. Then Veronica Earnshaw was shot while microchipping a pup without a clue to who was about to kill her. Next, Marian Foxcroft was attacked and hit on the head. Once we ID'd Carrie as the perp—at least on Melanie and the rookies' murders because of the crazy evidence in her home—a rifle came into play. Seems to me our Carrie, if it is her, is an equal opportunity assassin."

"You may have a valid point."

"Thanks. Some of us have discussed it and we agree. Nothing is beyond that woman. We can't expect her actions to make sense to us when her thinking is so distorted."

Ryder shivered. "It makes me queasy when I think of all the delicious baked goods and other food she brought to work. There could have been poison in any of it and we'd never have suspected until it was too late."

"Only if she could have made sure you didn't eat any," Shane reminded him. "As far as we know, she still thinks you belong to her and fate will bring you together."

"Yeah. Too bad for her that psychopaths are not my style."

Shane chuckled at the bad joke. "Right. You prefer women who are so independent and spunky they only ask for help as a last resort."

"I wouldn't go quite that far." Nevertheless, Ryder was smiling and looking in the direction of the training center, a quarter of a mile away. He sobered. "I was afraid I'd lost Sophie when that inflatable collapsed. It could have suffocated her if bystanders hadn't helped hold it up until we could pull her out."

"Did you hear what you just said? You said, '*I* could have lost her,' not *we*. Sounds pretty personal to me."

"Slip of the tongue," Ryder alibied.

Shane laughed as the door opened and the rookies who were coming off duty filed in. Gina was with them and went straight to her fiancé. It did Ryder's heart good to see the couple so happy. Once this special assignment was over and Shane transferred to a permanent position the way he'd planned, Gina would go with him and Sophie would be short an assistant. Would she leave, too?

That idea settled in Ryder's chest like a boulder. Without Sophie to tease and laugh with, he'd be nearly as bereft as he'd been after losing Melanie.

"Not a good sign," he muttered to himself.

The pizzas were delivered just as Shane asked, "What?" saving Ryder from having to answer, and by the time everyone had grabbed a slice and settled down to eat, he figured he was going to escape having to explain.

Then Sophie walked in. Not only did the conversation lag, all focus turned to her. She had not only spruced up, she had tied her hair back, leaving ringlets loose around her face. Her cheeks were a natural pink, her lipstick rosy and her hazel eyes sparkling.

Greeting the group, she ended with Ryder and gave him the most beautiful smile he had ever seen.

His face warmed, and he grinned back at her.

Judging by the whoops and catcalls from his officers and others, he wasn't the only one who had noticed the mutual reactions.

But *he* was the sole problem. Carrie had already proved she'd do anything to have him for herself, including murder. Any personal changes in his life would have to wait.

Ryder grabbed a half-empty pizza box and held it out to Sophie, keeping her from coming too close.

"Your steak, Ms. Williams?"

She accepted a slice, held it up and made a face. "Looks like a poor substitute to me. Titus would be very disappointed."

So am I, Ryder thought. Keeping his distance from the attractive trainer was getting harder and harder. He didn't mind if his staff noticed. All he needed to be sure of was that their growing attraction didn't spill over to their times in public and give a practiced murderer another target.

Okay, I did my best, Sophie told herself. Short of dressing in her church clothes, she'd spruced up well. At least she'd thought so. And Ryder's initial reaction had been favorable. So why had he shut down as though he was sorry he'd acted glad to see her?

She'd bided her time long enough for most of the others to leave before she cornered him to ask. "Can I have a word with you, Chief?"

He finished cleaning up napkins and stuffing them in the empty boxes before he said, "Sure. I'll run this out to the Dumpster so the office doesn't smell like an Italian restaurant. Be right back."

"You can do that later," she insisted.

Ryder's left eyebrow arched. "Are you giving me orders?"

"Since you seem to need them, yes," she said flatly. Her insides were quaking but as far as she could tell, it didn't show.

"My office."

She preceded him, sensing his presence as he followed closely. When he shut the door, she had reached the edge of his desk so she turned and perched there, intending to appear casual.

"What won't wait?" he demanded, hands fisted.

The words she'd been rehearsing for the past

hour deserted her and she was left with a disturbing void, both in thought and action. She clasped her hands in front of her. "Maybe this was a bad idea."

"Maybe it was. But I'm here now and I expect you to explain. Spit it out. What's on your mind?"

"You," she said honestly. "All the time. Night and day. On or off duty. And I wonder if I should have my head examined."

Ryder's slow progress toward her gave her hope—until he abruptly circled his desk, making it a barrier between them.

He sat, laced his fingers together on the desktop and looked up at her. "Has it occurred to you that by showing interest in me you are risking your life?"

Sophie rolled her eyes. "Oh, no, I never thought of that." Her voice rose. "Of *course* it's occurred to me."

"Then you understand."

"No. I don't. I can see not flaunting it but I'd sure like to know if my feelings are as far off base as Carrie's were. Do you like me or don't you?"

"Of course I like you."

The calmness of delivery and the lack of evident emotion in his affirmation made her wonder if he was merely being polite to placate a slightly unhinged coworker. That was certainly how it came across.

"Oooo-kay," she drawled. "And?"

Ryder took a deep breath and blew it out, apparently making a decision. "And, it is killing me to have to stay away from you."

"Really? Why didn't you *say* so?"

"Because…" He paused to study his folded hands, then went on, "Because I was afraid to."

"Afraid *for* me or *of* me?"

"Take your pick. If Carrie got wind of my interest in you she'd do all she could to eliminate her so-called competition. Maybe she's already started. Plus, if you didn't share my feelings or decided to move away from Desert Valley, I wasn't sure I'd survive. It was easier to keep my distance and let everything else work itself out first."

"Very logical. You must have green Vulcan blood, Chief."

He chuckled wryly. "Because I want you to live long and prosper?"

"Something like that." Feeling her courage swell as the seconds ticked by, Sophie approached him. "Stand up."

Cautiously, he got to his feet. She could see his breathing growing more rapid, his cheeks reddening. The handsome, powerful, commanding man did have gentle, loving traits. She'd seen them when he was working with the dogs. And it was even more evident when he spoke about Lily.

Her own heart fluttered. When Ryder had claimed he'd be hurt if she left, he had touched a nerve. It was one thing to be hugged after a near escape and quite another to share a quiet, mutual embrace.

Slipping her arms around his waist she took the last step and laid her cheek on his chest. The rapid pounding of his heart echoed that of her own speeding pulse. He didn't push her away, nor did he complete the affectionate gesture.

"Sophie, I..."

There were unshed tears in her eyes when she lifted her gaze and said, "If you aren't going to kiss me, at least give me a hug."

Ryder's arms tightened. She felt his warm breath on her hair, sensed him kissing her there. Until she had begun to fall for him she had not realized how lonely she was. Now? Now she was head over heels for a man who had been as lonely as she was and had only recently let down his guard. She didn't want to push him. She only wanted the affection she now knew he'd been withholding.

His hand stroked her cheek, his thumb whisking away a tear. He crooked a finger beneath her chin and lifted it.

Sophie had dreamed what his kiss would be like but her fantasy had fallen far short of reality. The touch of his lips was light, tender and warm, yet infused with a sense of love beyond anything she had ever imagined.

All too soon Ryder released her and stepped back. Resting his hands on her shoulders he said,

"There. Now you know how I feel. All I ask is that we bide our time before we try to explore our feelings for each other any more. Please, Sophie?"

The best she could do was nod. No wonder he'd worried about Carrie's jealousy. This was no simple fling. She and Ryder were falling in love.

Hiding that much serious emotion from a stalker and murderer was not going to be easy.

Could they? Sophie seriously doubted it.

FIFTEEN

The following week passed without incident. A cleanup crew made up of volunteers from Desert Valley service clubs and other helpful individuals had Main Street and the square swept and scrubbed, looking cleaner than it had before the homecoming.

Ryder was dreading having to send Lily back to school soon because that would mean she'd be vulnerable until he or Opal picked her up in the afternoon. Worse, the child had developed a case of hero worship regarding a certain female dog trainer. He didn't mind the crush; he simply wanted to keep his daughter away from any possible source of danger.

Right now, he felt as if he, himself, posed the biggest risk. He'd often been told that it was easy to see how much he cared for Sophie, whether he denied it or not. If his friends and staff could tell at a glance, it was likely that any observer could.

Still, there had been no local sightings of Carrie and the state police were clueless, too. That was a good sign providing she was gone—a bad sign if she wasn't.

Office hours were usually more of a suggestion than a rule, particularly concerning the law officers, and Ryder was often the last to leave.

This particular day he had told Opal he'd be late picking up Lily because he was going to work Phoenix in the evening. There were several reason for choosing that time. The first was to take advantage of less daytime distraction. The second was to keep from being noticed spending extra time with Sophie.

Unfortunately, Opal phoned just as he was leaving his office. "Hayes."

"I hate to bother you, Chief, but my sister in Mesa's been hauled to the hospital. She's a widow and I need to go be with her. Can you come get Lily now?"

Ryder sighed, disappointed. "Sure. I'll be there in a couple of minutes. Is there anything else I can do for you? Do you need a ride?"

"I drove a jeep in combat," Opal countered. "I think I can handle my own transportation. But thanks for asking."

"Well, if you need anything, just give a holler."

"I will. And while I'm gone, you might consider leaving Lily with Marilyn Martin. She already watches Shelby for Whitney Godwin. She's real good with kids and I hear her place is real nice."

"I'll think about it. I just have to cancel my appointment tonight and I'll be on my way."

"No real rush," the older woman told him. "I'm not packed yet."

"Okay. See you soon."

Assuming that Sophie had been looking forward to their training session as much as he had, Ryder decided to stop by the training center instead of phoning to cancel.

The moment he saw her begin to grin at him he wished he'd called. Seeing her enthusiasm for his presence and then having to turn around and leave was going to be disappointing.

"You're early," she said.

He nodded. "Something has come up. I can't make it tonight."

Sophie's arched eyebrows predicted argument. "Why not?"

"Opal has to leave town and can't watch Lily."

"Then bring her with you," Sophie countered. "You know she loves to work with the dogs. We can put her in the puppy pen and let them play while we train Phoenix."

"She would love that. I just..."

"Benny Sims will be on guard duty by the time the others leave. If you're nervous about it, keep one of your regulars around as backup. Eddie Harmon's always looking for overtime. Those six kids of his keep him broke."

"I suppose I could do that," Ryder said soberly.

"If I can get a second officer to stand guard tonight then okay, I'll be back with Lily. If not, try to understand?"

"I do." Sophie approached slowly and laid a warm hand on his forearm, sending electricity shooting up Ryder's spine. There was unspoken pleading in her gaze.

It was all he could do to keep from pulling her into his arms and kissing her over and over. Judging by the misty look in her hazel eyes she was having equal trouble resisting the urge for closeness—for the affection and total acceptance that had been missing from both their lives for all too long.

"My dogs are in the car. I hate to drive all the way home to drop off Titus. How about I bring him back with Phoenix? If tonight works out, I mean."

Her smile returned. "Sounds fine. Titus can nap while he's here."

Stepping away, she removed her hand from Ryder's arm and he immediately felt the loss. He'd make tonight work. He had to. Everything in his heart and mind insisted.

They'd train mostly inside, he reasoned, staying out of sight of the public and setting up tracking scenarios for Phoenix. Lily might even be able to help. The eager dog could track her the way he did at home when they played hide-and-seek. Both the dog and the child would love it.

Instead of going through dispatch, Ryder called Eddie personally. When he begged off due to a birthday party for one of his kids, Ryder contacted Dennis Marlton. He was free and agreed to work overtime.

That settled it. Elated, Ryder called the training center to assure Sophie he and Lily would be there. "I'll need to feed her," he told the trainer. "Are you up for another pizza? Lily's been asking for one ever since she found out she'd missed the feast we had at the station after the fair."

"Sure. I'm easy to please," Sophie said. Ryder could tell she was grinning as she spoke.

"Okay. It's a date. You get me, a spoiled rotten kid and two dogs, all to yourself."

"Sounds like the perfect combo," Sophie gibed.

Ryder hoped she'd still think so after Carrie was captured and they could meet openly and socialize like normal people.

He was no stranger to the kind of stressed friendships trouble often brought about. Nobody thought clearly in the middle of a traumatic situation, and although no one had taken potshots at any of his staff or the trainers lately, that didn't make the emotional upheaval go away. Only time, and the capture of their nemesis, would do that.

So, where was Carrie Dunleavy?

Instinct made him glance in his rearview mirrors. Nothing was out of place. Nobody was following him.

Nevertheless, he continued to watch. Letting down his guard now would be more foolish than walking into the line of fire without his bulletproof vest.

Sophie heard Lily coming before she saw her. The little girl was singing at the top of her lungs and skipping down the hallway. Titus followed obediently while Phoenix ran interference in front of her.

Bringing up the rear was the chief, carrying a pizza that reminded her how hungry she was. "Wow, that smells good. Glad to see you all made it."

"Everything been quiet around here?"

"Totally. Dennis is out back. You probably passed Benny when you came in."

"We did. Lily promised him a slice of pizza. I hope we don't starve after she gives all our dinner away."

"I doubt that will happen," Sophie said, chuckling and leading the way to her office. "Unless we step away from the box and a certain Australian shepherd helps himself."

"He's stopped stealing food at home," Ryder reported. "I won't guarantee that my softhearted daughter won't slip him something, though."

Sophie took a moment to caution Lily. "Onions

are bad for dogs and spices can sometimes hurt their tummies, so it's not a good idea to let them eat from the table." She made sure to keep smiling so the girl wouldn't feel too chastised. "I teach all the police dogs a special command about eating that helps keep them from getting poisoned. After we're done, I'll teach you how to feed him from your hand the right way. Okay?"

"Okay!"

"If I get you a paper plate do you think you can take Benny his piece by yourself?"

"Uh-huh."

Sophie prepared the plate, then cautioned Lily to use two hands while she and Ryder restrained the dogs. She caught him gazing fondly at his daughter as Lily walked away, taking great care to properly balance the flimsy plate.

"Kennel," she said, trusting Titus to obey but keeping a hand on Phoenix's collar just in case. To her delight, Ryder followed them. He'd stuffed his hands in his pockets and looked nonchalant but she figured he had to be at least as uneasy as she was.

Closing and latching the gate to the dog run she turned, not at all surprised to find him close behind. "Shall we get this over with so we can enjoy our meal," she asked.

"Get what over with?" His words may have been questioning but his facial expression was all-knowing.

"Another kiss," she said, noting added warmth that had nothing to do with the outside desert temperature.

"You liked the first one?" Ryder drawled.

"It was passable." That line would have been funnier if she'd been able to deliver it without giggling.

"Well, if you insist."

Sophie didn't need any more of an invitation. She slipped her arms around his neck and stood on tiptoe. There was no awkwardness, no hesitation. They kissed as if they had been practicing for years. Her only regret was that they had not.

It was Ryder who stopped them. "I suggest we cool it. Lily is already wondering when I'm going to get her another mother. Opal planted the idea."

Speechless, Sophie averted her gaze. *Mother?* That meant marriage, and although she was pretty sure she was in love with Ryder she wasn't convinced she'd be a good mother for anybody. She certainly hadn't grown up with an adequate role model. Was it possible to learn to be a good parent or did a person have to absorb it via experience?

She broke away and headed back toward her office. Not only was the pizza still there, Lily was already picking bits of sausage off the top.

"Hey," Ryder called. "No fair. You have to share with us, too."

Instead of smiling the way Sophie had expected

her to, Lily made a grumpy face, said, "Whatever" and plopped down into a chair with her arms crossed.

The moment Sophie's eyes met Ryder's she knew. They both did. The little girl had come back before they had expected her to and had seen them kissing. That had to be why she was pouting, since nothing else unusual had taken place.

"I'll get you a plate and your own serving," Ryder said. "Which one do you want?"

"I'm not hungry."

"Fine. It can sit here until you are. Sophie and I are going to eat."

Ryder seemed to make a point of keeping his distance after that. Sophie fully understood. It didn't matter if the child had voiced a desire for a new mother, seeing her daddy paying special attention to any woman had to be a shock. After all, Lily had had Ryder all to herself her entire life.

I can love her through it, Sophie decided. *No parent is perfect. If I do my best and take advice from women with experience, like Opal, I'll be a good mother.*

Providing Ryder doesn't decide to drop me to make Lily happy, she added sadly. That was always a possibility. Her own parents had chosen to abandon her so why should anybody else behave differently?

This is a terrible way to think, Sophie told herself. She already had a good, productive life and a career she loved. If God didn't choose to bless her with more, so be it.

The pizza began to taste like cardboard and she was barely able to choke it down. One look at Lily told her the five-year-old wasn't in any better mood than she was.

Poor Ryder. His efforts at placating his daughter weren't working, and now his supposed girlfriend was moping, too. The guy had to be at his wit's end.

And, as Sophie had learned long ago, the best antidote for a bad mood was spending time with dogs. They loved without question and commiserated when necessary.

Catching Ryder's eye, Sophie nodded toward the kennel area. "Weren't you going to show Lily the new puppies?"

"That's right. I was." He reached for her hand and gave enough of a tug to draw her to her feet. "You get the training session ready while we go look at pups."

"Gladly." It was Sophie's fondest hope that the father would use his time alone with his daughter to try to smooth things over, although it might be better to wait and let Lily adjust slowly.

Or not at all. Sophie wanted to slap herself for having such negative thoughts. Normally, she was far more upbeat. More self-confident. That happened when she felt comfortable and in her element with the dogs. People were another thing altogether. Hard to understand. Unpredictable and untrustworthy. They had been for as long as she could remember.

Some, like Carrie Dunleavy, were more than that, she concluded. They weren't just unknowable. They were evil to the core.

She shivered. The building was deserted except for her and the Hayes family. And the dogs, she reminded herself. Always the dogs. The one—the only—reliable element in her life.

Ryder thought about having a serious talk with Lily and decided against it. At this point they only suspected what was wrong with the girl. If he brought up his tender feelings for Sophie and that wasn't the reason Lily was sulking, he'd be adding to her melancholy.

"Stay in here with the puppies as long as you like," Ryder told her. "I'll put Titus right next to you and I'll be in the training room teaching Phoenix how to track for search and rescue."

"He already knows," Lily grumbled. "I taught him."

"I know you've played that game. What we need to do now is make sure he knows what we want when we tell him and can pick out the right scents."

"He's not as smart as Titus."

"They're both good dogs," Ryder argued, giving the arthritic old dog a clean blanket to lie on. "You were too young to remember what Titus was like when I first got him but he had to learn, too. For the same reasons you have to start back to school soon."

"I don't wanna go to school. I wanna stay with Opal."

Was *that* what was bothering Lily? "Well, you can't do that right now so get over it. Opal's sister needs her."

"I don't want a sister. Ever," Lily declared, surprising Ryder again. This was a kid who had once begged him to get her a baby sister or brother. Clearly, nothing he said or did was going to please her tonight. Actually, she reminded him of Melanie; like on the night she was killed. He had had to work late and rather than wait a few minutes for him to give her a ride, she had stomped off toward home, carrying the fancy dress she'd picked up at the cleaners.

Remembering that detail wasn't enough to smash all his guilt but it did put a serious dent in it. If Melanie had waited for him she might have lived, at least then. Given Carrie's mental illness, she would probably have found a way to eliminate his wife eventually, no matter what he had done or not done.

Which reminded him of Sophie. After closing

and latching the kennel gates he hurried back to her.

"How's she doing?" Sophie asked, clearly concerned.

"She's sulking because Opal had to go away, I think. I'm either going to bring Lily to work with me or put her in that day care Marilyn Martin runs."

"I understand Whitney uses her so she must be fine."

"That's what Opal said. I just have a terrible time letting go. It's as if I'm seeing Melanie in Lily and wondering how long it will be before I lose her, too."

"I see."

Ryder cupped her shoulders. "I don't think you do. I'm not looking for another Melanie. It's worrisome enough to see Lily acting so much like her mother."

"I thought you two were happy."

"We were. But we were young and headstrong. The time we had together was cut short before we'd really come to terms with a shared life. I'd hoped having a baby would mellow us both out."

"And then you had to raise her all alone."

He nodded. "Yes. Opal taught me a lot. She was a good influence on Lily. I just wonder if she hasn't spoiled her."

A knowing grin spread across Sophie's face. "And you haven't?"

When Ryder's pager buzzed, he considered it a rescue from having to admit a fault. He checked in by radio, then told Sophie, "There's a major traffic accident out on the westbound."

"Will you have to leave?"

"No. I'm not needed. We may eventually have to kick Marlton loose, but I'm not going anywhere."

The look of relief on Sophie's pretty face warmed his heart. She wasn't the kind of woman who would resent him for doing his duty, but it was evident she wanted him to stick around. That was the best of both worlds. Someone who yearned for his company, yet was willing to let him go without pitching a fit.

That had been another sore point between him and his late wife, Ryder recalled. Melanie loved him. But she didn't want to share.

Just like Carrie Dunleavy.

SIXTEEN

It pleased Sophie when Phoenix successfully followed a scented drag through the building to the box where she'd hidden it.

"He's good," Ryder commented, giving the dog's silky ears a scratch and patting him on the head.

"I think he's great. How about trying him outside?"

"It's too well lit."

"That's what switches are for," Sophie teased. "When they're flipped up, lights come on. When you flip them down, the lights go off. Trust me. I can make it dark in the yard."

Ryder gave her a look of disgust. "You have a serious problem with your sense of humor, lady. It's warped."

"You're just now noticing?" To her delight, he laughed softly.

"Tell you what," she said. "How about seeing if Lily wants to be our missing person and hide while I give Phoenix a drink of water and let him rest?"

"Not out there. In here. I'm not comfortable with risking her or the dog in the training yard."

"Not even with the lights off?"

Ryder shook his head. "Not even with the lights off."

"Okay. Have it your way. I'll make a pass through to check with Benny and Officer Marlton, then hold Phoenix back there until you're ready."

"Where shall I hide her? In the keyhole under your desk?"

Sophie was chuckling as she clamped her hands over both of the Aussie's ears. "Shush. Don't tell him."

"Right. You think he understands English?"

"Some. He headed right for my refrigerator the first time I mentioned food."

"That's not really as ridiculous as it sounds. Titus knows Lily by name."

"Of course he does. When I was a kid, I had to spell to keep my dog from figuring out what I was doing. He was my best friend."

"Dog friend, you mean."

Sophie gave him a wistful smile and explained. "No. Any friend. He lived up to the name Buddy all the time. He even defended me from my own parents a few times." She waved her hands in front of her as if erasing her words. "Forget I said that."

The wary look in Ryder's eyes as he turned to

go get his daughter convinced Sophie he would never forget her telling admission; one, because it had shocked him and two, because it was part of her background and would undoubtedly affect her for the rest of her life. She had learned to be wary. Untrusting. And cautious beyond normal boundaries due to her dysfunctional upbringing. If nothing else kept him from regarding her as a potential mate, that would.

Remembering how Shane had managed to overlook Gina's mentally unbalanced fraternal twin brother and form a lasting relationship made Sophie both happy and sad. She was happy that two nice people had found each other, yet sad that she, herself, felt so isolated and alone.

"It's high time for a puppy session," she told herself, hoping Lily had received the same kind of emotional relief by keeping company with the exuberant youngsters. If anything could lift spirits it was a lap full of warm, squirmy pups.

There had been times when her predecessor, Veronica, had caught Sophie sitting on the floor of one of the runs, laughing and letting puppies crawl all over her. Such behavior had not pleased the inflexible head trainer but Sophie had continued to do it during her breaks, anyway. It was a good way to socialize the dogs and the best antidote for loneliness.

Speaking of which... She checked her watch and wondered if she should make another round between the two guards just for something to do. Neither had reported any problems and Benny had even been awake when she'd contacted him.

Although she and Ryder had only been apart for a few minutes, Sophie missed him terribly. Judging by the tension in Phoenix's leash, he did, too. That was a good sign. They had obviously bonded as handler and K-9 should. Instinct had told her they'd be perfect for each other so that was a gold star for her, too. She knew she had a gift for making successful pairings the same as Veronica had, only in Sophie's case she did it more by gut feelings than by strict rules. Thankfully, her junior trainer, Gina Perry agreed. Good training was part science, part intuition.

Sophie shivered. If Carrie had been a mad dog instead of a human murderer, she might have discerned enough to have stopped her years ago.

And now? Now, it was no secret that Carrie was guilty. The senses Sophie needed now were ones that would telegraph danger in time to head it off.

The problem was, all the previous attacks had left her so jumpy she no longer trusted her own sensations of apprehension and fear.

Such as those which she was feeling right now.

Ryder found his daughter curled up on the clean blanket with Titus. She had apparently tired of the rambunctious puppies and had let herself out so she could join the more peaceful dog. His ribs rose gently with each breath and cradled Lily's head as they both snoozed.

The dog detected him, opened one eye and thumped his tail. Crouching, Ryder petted him. "Good boy."

God, please watch over Lily, Ryder prayed silently. He had always said special prayers for his only child but lately they had become a lot more frequent and tinged with a touch of desperation. If he was this worried about her well-being at five, what would it be like when she was fifteen?

Titus's panting awoke Lily. She rubbed her eyes. "Can we go home now?"

"Pretty soon," her father told her. "I want to stay in town a little longer. There's a bad wreck out on the highway and they may need me."

"Oh." Cuddling against the warm dog she closed her eyes again.

"Would you like to help us train?" Ryder asked.

"No."

"You can hide and let Phoenix find you."

"Uh-uh."

"There's pizza left, too," he added, slightly relieved when she sat up. "We could warm it for you."

"Can Titus come, too?"

Ryder wasn't about to argue. "Sure. You can give him your crusts as long as you eat all the good stuff off first."

"*She* said *no*." Lily glared toward the offices.

"That was for Phoenix. Titus is going to be staying home with us more from now on so we can treat him like a pet."

"Okay." The child was on her feet, stretching and yawning, in seconds. To Ryder's amusement, the old dog mimicked her. Letting Titus trail them he took Lily's hand. "How did you manage to get the gates open? I thought you were too short."

"I'm big."

"You certainly are. But that catch is outside."

"It was open already."

"That's impossible."

She shook her blond curls. "Uh-uh. It was open. All I had to do was jump up and knock the handle over."

Doing his best to mute his disbelief, he continued to press her. "What about the one for Titus?"

"It wasn't fastened, either."

"Okay." Leading her back to the office, he remembered that Sophie was waiting out of sight with Phoenix. She'd been in the kennels after he had clipped those gate latches. Maybe she'd undone them without thinking. He'd ask her ASAP. In the meantime, he had a test to set up and a hungry child to finally feed.

"Do you want your pizza nuked?" Ryder asked Lily.

"No. That makes it too hot to eat. Titus doesn't like it that way."

Ryder had to smile. "All right. We need to

find a good place for both of you to hide so Titus doesn't tell Phoenix where you are."

"I know." Lily brightened. "Upstairs!"

"I'm not sure that's a good idea."

"Awwww."

"Sophie is right. I'm a sucker for you," he muttered. "Okay. Bring your supper and follow me. I'm not letting you go up there without checking it, first."

"You'll stink up the trail," Lily said wisely.

She may have put it crudely but she was right. "Then you'd better pick a place down here, because I'm not going to let you hide until I check where you'll be."

Lily tiptoed across the room and peeked into one of the large crates they used for training.

It was going to be an easy tracking task but at least it was safe, Ryder reasoned. "That's perfect. You and Titus get inside and be very quiet. And don't let him steal your supper."

"Okay, Daddy."

A grin spread across Ryder's face as he left to fetch Sophie. He didn't have the keen senses of a tracking dog but even a human could smell that aromatic slice of pizza. If Phoenix failed this test he belonged on a farm herding sheep the way his ancestors had.

After a glance back to be sure all was well, he left the room. By the time he reached Sophie his pager had sounded again. The officers at the wreck were asking for more backup and additional ambulances.

Sobering, he greeted her smile with a frown. "What's wrong? Is Lily okay?"

"She's fine. Eating, actually. But I may have to cut Marlton loose to respond to that earlier collision. Apparently the pileup was hit again by at least two speeders and it's pretty bad out there."

Sophie gently touched his arm. "Do you have to go, too?"

"I hope not." He managed a lopsided smile for her benefit. "Come on. Bring Wonder Mutt. If he can't find a kid eating pizza and hiding with another dog, he's not the search and rescue tracker we'd hoped."

"I'm not worried."

Neither was Ryder. At least not about the K-9's tracking abilities. He had plenty of other things on his mind that kept his gut tied in knots. Such as whether he was neglecting his sworn duty by not responding to the multivehicle accident. Recent reports had specified needing more traffic control, not another chief officer. If that changed, he'd have to leave Lily behind for her own good. No way was he taking his little girl to a grisly accident scene.

Sophie had concerns about the victims of the traffic collision and had silently prayed for them when the first reports had come in. She had faith in the first responders, too. Desert Valley law officers and firefighters had a sterling record. They were extraordinary, particularly for such a small town.

She led the way back to the office area and paused at her desk. "Do you want me to use the pizza aroma or do you have something of Lily's for Phoenix to smell?"

Ryder presented a small, pink sweater. "Here you go. She keeps insisting she's not cold but she was curled up with Titus on a blanket out back."

"Cute. You should have snapped a picture with your phone," Sophie said, smiling. "Stand back. Here we go."

Instructing the dog to sit and watch her, she carefully presented the sweater and let him sniff it thoroughly. Then she commanded, "Seek."

In her peripheral vision Sophie saw Ryder shift. She was the one who was supposed to be nervous, not him, and she was amused until he shouted, "Hey!"

"What's the matter?"

"He's going the wrong way. Lily's in that crate over there."

"Well, she has walked through here several times tonight. It's a forgivable mistake. Let's let him sort out the newest scents from the previous ones." Giving the dog his head, she let him take her where he would. "This is one reason I thought we should do the test outside. She hadn't been running around in the training yard today."

Phoenix cast back and forth in a sweeping motion, moving forward with care. Ryder's pacing and fidgeting was beginning to get to her. "Stand still, will you? I'd be confused, too, if I thought you were trying to direct me and the instructions went contrary to what my nose was telling me."

"He's way off."

"Fine. Then we'll end this before you come unglued. Go get your pizza lover and bring her out."

As Sophie restrained Phoenix, Ryder jogged across the room and bent over the crate. When he straightened a moment later, his face was ashen and his eyes wide. "She's gone."

"What do you mean, gone? Are you sure that's where you put her?"

"Of course I'm sure." He spun in a full circle.

Sophie had already approached the crate and redirected Phoenix by the time Ryder said, "Turn the dog loose."

More urging wasn't necessary. The Aussie was almost pulling her off her feet as she struggled to unclip the long leash. His straining reminded her of a sled dog in an Alaska race.

Phoenix would have knocked Ryder down if he hadn't jumped aside. Once the dog struck the new scent trail, he careened around furniture and bounded up the stairs to the second story.

"I told her *not* to go up there," Ryder shouted.

He was so close behind when he yelled, he startled Sophie into stumbling. The excited canine disappeared around the corner at the top of the stairs in a blur.

Sophie yearned to be able to assure Ryder his child was safe but she kept silent. All she managed to mutter was, "Please, Jesus," over and over.

They topped the staircase at the same time. If Ryder had not grabbed her arm she might have been knocked down in his rush to shoulder past her.

"Lily! Lily, where are you?" he called.

Sophie raised her free hand. "Shush. Listen."

"I don't hear a thing."

"That's because you're making so much noise," she countered. Now that she was back on solid flooring she shook loose from his grasp.

"Where's that fool dog," Ryder roared, racing from room to room of the small, converted apartment.

Sophie stifled a grin and paused to catch her breath. For a guy who was the epitome of a calm, cool, sensible police chief, he was a basket case as a father. She snagged his arm when he ran past for the second time. "Stop!"

"I have to…"

"You have to stop and think and listen," she said, keeping her voice soft so he'd have to be quiet or miss what she was saying. "I hear giggling."

"I don't."

"Hold your breath before you hyperventilate. I think both dogs may be hiding with Lily. That's why we can't see Phoenix."

Ryder released the air in his lungs with a whoosh. His shoulders sagged. "I hear it, too, now."

Bending over and resting his hands on his knees, he continued to gasp as if no amount of air was enough.

Sophie placed a hand of comfort on his back and called, "You win, Lily. You and the dogs fooled your daddy."

The child didn't pop out of hiding but her laughter increased, soon to be accompanied by a bass woof from the old Lab and a tenor whine from Phoenix.

As soon as Sophie opened the closet where she stored equipment, all three tumbled out.

Titus plopped down on the rug, panting. Phoenix bounded around the room. Lily emerged, laughing and clapping hands sporting traces of tomato sauce, then ran straight to her father.

Ryder dropped to his knees, arms open to her, eyes glistening.

Sophie didn't want to embarrass him but she couldn't look away. The sight of father and daughter together was too precious, too awe inspiring.

What would it be like to be loved that much?

To have a parent who truly cared?

* * *

Ryder wanted to scold his little girl but he simply could not bring himself to do it. He was too glad to see her. And too ashamed of his show of weakness in front of Sophie. She must think he was a raving lunatic, like Gina's brother Tim had been when they'd apprehended him. Of all the times in his life when he'd been caught off-kilter, this was the first incidence where he'd lost his perspective. All he'd been able to think about was finding Lily the way he'd found Melanie. For a few terrible moments he'd thought that tragedy was happening again.

His cell phone rang as they were all making their way back down the stairs. Because he was carrying Lily on one hip he let it go to voice mail.

"You should get that," Sophie said.

"I will. Just give me a second." *A year would be better*, he thought, chagrined. Raising this child was bound to have turned him gray by then, not that it would stand out in his blond hair.

He gave her another squeeze. She protested. "Da-a-a-d. I'm not a baby."

"You don't act very grown-up, young lady. I told you not to go upstairs."

"You said it needed to be checked. So I took Titus." She beamed at the old dog. "He did a good job, huh?"

"I hope so," Ryder said.

His attempt to hand Lily off to Sophie met with

little arms wrapping more tightly around his neck so he pulled out his phone and sat with the child on his lap. The voice mail message required a prompt reply.

Eyeing Sophie, he paused. "Sounds like they do need another chief after all. Opal's long gone by now. Any chance you can look after Lily for me? I shouldn't be out there long."

The child wailed, "No, Daddy. I'll be good. I promise."

"This has nothing to do with not obeying me," Ryder insisted. "An active accident scene is no place for kids. The officers and paramedics on scene need me to coordinate evacuation of the latest victims. It's not only ugly out there, it's not safe for you."

Instead of listening to reason, Lily wailed. "Nooooo."

"The dogs are staying here with Sophie," he offered. "Don't you want to be with Titus?"

She did him the favor of a sniffle and a nod.

"Well, then, get down and let me return this call. The sooner I go and do my job, the sooner I'll be back."

"You always leave."

"And I come back. Remember that, honey." If she had been old enough to have remembered Melanie he thought she might have argued, but she didn't. A baby whose mother hadn't been around to raise her was bound to be confused despite Opal's heroic efforts as a surrogate.

How hard might it be for Lily to accept a younger substitute? he wondered. Perhaps someone like Sophie. They certainly seemed compatible. And he felt affection for her. She was not only loving and understanding, she was fun to be around. Her approach to life might be a tad odd but it was never dull.

Ryder bent and stared into his daughter's beautiful blue eyes. "All right, Lily. This is how it's going to be. I'm going to go out to the accident scene and you're going to stay here with Titus, Phoenix and Sophie. Period."

She hung her head. "Yes, Daddy." Eyes widening, she apparently thought of an excuse. "What if I get tired? Where will I sleep?"

"You seemed to do just fine bunking with Titus in the kennel. If Ms. Sophie says you can sleep inside, you have my permission to keep both dogs with you."

"And the puppies?"

He could tell Sophie was struggling to keep a straight face. "Don't push it," Ryder said with a smile. "Two will give you one dog to pet with each hand."

"What about my toes?"

Sophie's shoulders were shaking and she'd pressed a hand over her mouth.

"Toes don't count unless we're on the sofa at home and Titus is lying in front of it."

"Why not?"

"Because you have to wear shoes here and your toes are inside."

"Uh-uh." She held up a foot. "Sandals. See?"

Ryder realized she had outmaneuvered him and stopped trying to be logical. He crouched to look her straight in the eyes. "Lily. You will stay with Sophie while I'm gone and behave yourself because I say so. Understand?"

Curly blond hair fell in cascades and masked Lily's rosy cheeks as she bowed her head and said, "Yes, Daddy."

Ryder looked to Sophie. "If she gives you any trouble you can call me on my cell."

"I'm sure that won't be necessary."

"I hope not. Benny's still on the front door and Marlton's in the rear so you should be fine."

"I'll take good care of her," Sophie vowed.

He dropped his chief's persona long enough to say, "I know you will. I trust you."

The thing that surprised Ryder the most when he said that was the depth of truth in his words. He was entrusting his precious child to Sophie Williams and was less worried than he'd ever been when leaving Lily with Opal.

Promising himself he'd sort out that epiphany later, he headed for his patrol car. Suffering strangers needed his help. His family would be fine until he returned.

Family? Yes, he concluded. He had begun to view Sophie as the third member and realized he was finally at peace with that.

Forty-five minutes later, while directing an evacuation helicopter's landing, Ryder remembered he'd forgotten to ask Sophie about the unlatched gates.

SEVENTEEN

"What would you like to do?" Sophie asked Lily.

The pouting child merely shrugged.

"Are you still hungry? There's a little more pizza. How about a bottle of water? Aren't you thirsty"

A shake of the head.

Sophie made a face and blew a noisy sigh. "If you were a puppy I'd take you to the vet to see why you were acting so sad. But since you're not, and you can talk if you want to, I'll pick what we do." She looked around. "Let's see, there are dog bowls to wash and rinse. Or we could get down on our hands and knees and scrub cement with brushes so it's nice and clean for the next new dogs."

"Yuck."

"You have a better idea?"

Lily yawned. "We could play hide-and-seek."

"We could if we weren't all so tired. Titus is asleep and Phoenix is resting." She knew better than to list the weary child and trigger more argument. "Why don't we go upstairs to the break room and watch videos?"

"Cartoons?"

"Something better," Sophie told her. "You like dogs. I have some great training DVDs up there. And a sofa where you can sit with your shoes off and pet Titus with your toes."

"I can take my shoes off? Daddy said…"

"I know he did. But if you don't get up and walk around, sitting on this couch should be no different than the one you have at home."

To Sophie's relief and guarded delight, Lily looked happier. "Okay."

So far, so good. Their evening wasn't going to be all smiles, she knew, but this was a fair start at making peace. After all, she wasn't the child's mother so she really had no authority other than what Ryder had imparted when he'd left them together.

Lily rousted Titus, and Phoenix followed without hesitation. They had no trouble staking out positions next to the upstairs sofa as soon as Lily sat down and kicked off her shoes. Titus claimed his spot at her feet, laid his chin on his front paws and made himself at home. Less self-assured, Phoenix edged in next to the old dog until Sophie started the video player and joined the child. Then he took up a position by her feet.

"I like German shepherds," Lily said. "Why is that one so mean?"

"Because he's trained to act that way when he's on duty," Sophie explained. "Watch for a minute and you'll see how nice he is when he's at home."

"Titus is never mean."

"Dogs are like people." Smiling, Sophie patted Lily's knee. "Some are better at one job than any other. For instance, your daddy is good at catching bad guys."

"Yeah. He's real brave."

"I know. You must be very proud of him."

"Uh-huh."

"What's your favorite thing to do?"

"Tickle Titus." She raised a bare foot and giggled. "See?"

"I do see. He likes it, too."

"Yeah. Sometimes he licks my toes. The puppies did that tonight."

"I'm sure they did." Sophie began to relax. If she and Lily found nothing else to talk about, they could always fall back on their love of dogs. She cupped a hand around her mouth and leaned closer. "Can I tell you a secret?"

"Uh-huh." The sky blue eyes widened in anticipation.

"When it's really hot out and I'm hosing down the kennels, I sometimes take my shoes off and let the dogs chase my toes, too."

Lily covered her giggle. "I'll tell Daddy."

"That's okay. I don't mind." Remembering their water fight made Sophie grin. "When you do, ask him if he ever likes to play in the hose, okay?"

"Okay." Yawns were soon followed by a nodding head. Sophie slipped an arm around the child and let her doze close to her side. It was getting easier and easier to picture herself as a mother in spite of her own childhood woes. This wasn't so bad. It actually felt good to protect and shelter as if she were a mother hen tucking a chick beneath her wing. There was a Bible passage in Psalms about believers being tucked under God's wings. How did it go? "He shall cover you with His feathers and under His wings shall thou trust…"

Peace descended. Sophie was determined to stay awake despite the armed guards at both doors but her eyelids were growing heavy.

The DVD ended and apparently shut itself off, because when Sophie awoke the room was dark except for moonlight shining through the windows. The TV was silent. It took her a few seconds to realize that the warm creature half on, half off her lap was Lily.

Blinking to adjust to the dimness, Sophie was puzzled. Hadn't she left more lights burning? What about the hallway? The stairs?

A low rumble from the floor at the end of the couch came from Phoenix. She dropped her left hand and arm over the side and touched his silky fur. "What is it, boy?"

He slowly rose. Sophie kept her hand on him. "Easy. Stay." Although his muscles knotted he didn't leave her.

Easing aside to stand, she laid the sleeping child flat on the sofa cushions. There was a spare leash in the closet but Sophie knew better than to let go of the Aussie. Thankfully, he wasn't barking yet or he'd have awakened every dog in the place— and Lily, who was far less trouble than usual at the moment.

Keeping a hand on Phoenix's collar Sophie walked him to the storage closet where Lily had hidden earlier and located a leash. Once he was under control she led him to the top of the stairs. His nails clicked on the hard floor.

Sophie stopped. If the building's depths had not been so dark she wouldn't have been concerned. Power sometimes failed during storms, of course, but the weather had been mild lately.

One hand on the banister, the other holding the leash, she descended. From the main floor it was possible to see that other buildings obviously had electricity. So did the police department a quarter of a mile down Desert Valley Road. Did they have their own generator for emergencies?

"It doesn't matter," Sophie murmured. "What I want to know is why *this* place went dark."

The front door was the closest so she approached it. "Benny? Are you there?"

Louder. "Benny! Answer me. Are you okay?"

A hand in front of Phoenix's nose and a stern, "Stay" freed both hands. She drew her sidearm and released the safety on it before trying the door and finding it locked.

Sophie held her breath, turned the dead bolt and slowly opened the metal exterior door. The sidewalk outside was deserted. The only sign that Benny had been there was a half-empty soda bottle and a folding chair. She had known him to nap on the job but would never have dreamed he'd desert his post.

Phoenix was growling. He had stayed put, swiveling his head to look into the depths of the silent building.

She did the same, considering her options. If she left the area at the foot of the stairs, that would leave Lily open to attack from below. However, if she went to check on Marlton and found him, with or without Benny, she'd have reinforcements.

Because she had already called out and revealed her presence, she felt no reluctance to use her cell phone to inform Ryder of the strange situation. The call went straight to his voice mail. *911? No.* Not when so many officers and others were busy saving lives on the highway. She could handle this herself. She knew the layout of each room well enough to navigate without having to see well and the skylight in the indoor training area let in available moonlight. Plus, she was armed and had a dog with her. That magnified her human senses immeasurably.

Actually, given the situation, Sophie's decision was fairly easy. She'd get a flashlight, tell Marlton to check the fuse box and make sure all was well there, then contact the power company if the problem was not due to a fault in the training center's wiring.

An unexpected meow perked up the dog's ears. There was a *cat* in here? How in the world had that happened?

Sophie had not planned to release Phoenix. He had other ideas. He lunged. She lost her grasp on the leash. In a heartbeat he had outrun the beam of the flashlight and disappeared.

"Well, at least he can't get out," she grumbled, wishing she'd brought steady, predictable Titus with her before she concluded he was exactly where he belonged, upstairs guarding Lily.

Poor little kitty. It sure had picked the wrong building to invade. As soon as she'd gotten the electricity restored, Sophie planned to locate and save it from being overrun by canines. Most of them probably wouldn't hurt it but there were a few who might try, particularly if it was as young as it sounded.

Listening carefully, Sophie was puzzled that Phoenix was using a silent pursuit. That wasn't at all like him. Matter of fact, his barking was sometimes excessive.

The hair on the back of her neck prickled. "Phoenix? Phoenix, come."

No response. No barking, or whining. No sharp tapping of nails on the hard floor or scrambling sounds when he rounded a corner too fast and slipped.

Bile rose in Sophie's throat. Fright touched every nerve and demanded she run. As a dog trainer, her first responsibility was to the canines in her care, and if Lily had not been asleep upstairs she would have bravely pressed forward in search of the dog.

The presence of the helpless little girl changed everything. Phoenix had his speed and his teeth and the self-preservation instincts of an intelligent animal. Lily had nothing but an old dog and her; the woman who had vowed to keep her safe.

Wheeling, Sophie headed back toward the stairway. She had barely taken two steps when a searing pain cut through her head.

She remained conscious only long enough to feel herself starting to fall.

Then, blackness.

"Was that the last chopper?" reporter Madison Coles asked Ryder.

"Yes." He was hoping she wasn't going to take advantage of her relationship with rookie James Harrison to try to pick his brain for the *Canyon County Gazette*. A catastrophe like the one tonight was not something Ryder wanted to remember, let alone discuss.

"When you have a minute, you need to come see something, Chief," Harrison said. "One of the paramedics spotted it when he was cutting a victim loose with the Jaws of Life."

"What is it?"

"Take a look."

Ryder frowned, then crouched and began to clear scraps of debris off the object. It was about six inches wide and so long it disappeared beneath other wreckage. "A spike strip?"

"Looks like it to me. I wonder if the highway boys were in pursuit and laid it to stop whoever they were chasing?"

"I don't know. But I'm sure going to find out." He headed for the makeshift command post that had been set up in one of the patrol units parked safely off the road. A variety of uniforms showed the full complement of services that had been called in.

"Did one of you guys lay a spike strip?"

Denials were swift and loud.

Ryder held up both hands, palms forward. "That's what I figured. One of my men showed me something that sure looks as though there was nothing accidental about this pileup tonight. Somebody planned it."

As he spoke, a shiver shot up his spine. Who did he know who had the warped, evil mind necessary for such a horrible act? Who would harm innocent people like this? And why?

The *who* was easy. Carrie Dunleavy. But why? The only thing he could think of was creating a ruse to draw him and his men out of town. Carrie had never done anything without a reason. Even though it had taken years to figure out her twisted motives, they did exist. And they'd made a sick kind of sense once he'd seen the pictures and read her journal.

"Listen," Ryder announced, pointing to James. "This is Officer Harrison. He'll show you the device. I need to go."

The others were too focused on seeing the spikes to offer thanks. Ryder didn't care. He didn't need or want gratitude. What he wanted was to return to his daughter—and to Sophie—and hug them both as long and hard as possible.

Just because there had been no sightings of Carrie lately didn't mean she wasn't around. Criminal profilers in Flagstaff had warned she wouldn't go far. If they had been right, maybe she was in Desert Valley now.

Would she sabotage a highway just to get to him? Sure she would. She'd killed and maimed before. Stepping up her game after her crimes had been revealed made sense. She was running out of time. Out of opportunity. And hopefully, out of freedom.

He slid into his cruiser and flipped on the lights

and siren, then made a U-turn in the median and sped back toward town. If his ideas were wrong, there would be no harm done.

If he was right and Carrie was on the offensive, he'd need more than mere speed. He'd need divine guidance and protection for his loved ones. Lots of it.

Sophie heard moaning before realizing it was coming from her. Dizzy and disoriented she touched her aching scalp. Blood made her fingers sticky. She tried to sit up and failed to find good balance.

"Well, well, look who's finally coming around," a bitter-sounding woman said. "I should have saved Marian Foxcroft's silver poodle statue to use on you, too."

Sophie could hardly breathe. *That voice. It had to belong to whom she thought. Did she dare even speak the name?*

Wide-eyed, she fought to focus despite the bright beam of the discarded flashlight. Starting by noting low-heeled pumps, she observed tailored beige slacks and a plain brown blouse that almost matched the woman's mousy hair. Everything was familiar except the menacing glare in Carrie's eyes. And the pistol she was pointing.

Sophie's gaze narrowed to the hole in the end of the barrel. "That's my gun."

"It certainly is. Kind of you to provide it, dear.

I usually have to improvise, particularly since it's hard to lug a rifle around with me. Too conspicuous." She chuckled. "My aim is getting considerably better, don't you think?"

"You don't want to shoot me," Sophie offered, trying to reason with the madwoman.

"Why not? Do you think I don't know what you've been up to with my fiancé."

"I'm not up to anything, Carrie. Honest I'm not. All I care about is my dogs." A swell of panic almost closed her throat. "You, you didn't hurt any of them, did you?"

"Not yet. If you behave yourself I may not have to, either. Of course if you misbehave there are no guarantees. You saw what happened to Veronica, thanks to me. You should have celebrated. I got you a promotion."

There it was. The admission. Carrie Dunleavy had killed Veronica Earnshaw, Sophie's predecessor. The question was why. Veronica hadn't been interested in Ryder romantically. And he didn't particularly like her as a person, which would have made Carrie happy. So why had she killed her?

"You want my thanks for killing someone in cold blood?" The woman was insane.

Carrie nodded. "It might have been nice to get a little recognition for all the things I did at the police station. But no. Everybody ate my lovely baked goods and acted as if they expected me to keep treating them. Who ever treated me? Huh? Who? Even those mutts of yours didn't like me. Thank goodness I had my sweet kitties."

Two and two suddenly added up to four. "Did you bring a cat in here tonight to confuse the dogs?"

"Who, me?" Carrie meowed melodiously. "I didn't need to. My imitation was good enough to fool that stupid gray dog without endangering an innocent kitty. He ran through the back door and I locked him out." She cackled hoarsely. "He can keep those dumb guards company."

"Are they all right?"

Carrie shrugged. "Who knows!"

Sophie stared at her. "Why did you kill Veronica?"

"Boring question. But I have one. What I want to know is what happened to the girl."

"What girl?"

Carrie howled and raised the gun as if she were going to use it to backhand Sophie. "You know very well what girl. My daughter-to-be. Lily Hayes."

EIGHTEEN

Sophie felt helpless. Her head throbbed from behind her eyes to the base of her skull. The pain was not only nauseating, it kept her from thinking clearly.

How could this have happened? She'd been cautious to a fault. So had Ryder, even posting double the usual guards. If not for the traffic accident tonight he would have been there, too. What else could they possibly have done?

She supposed he could have shipped Lily out of town but his theory that the child was safer there with them was valid. He couldn't very well lock up his little girl while a crazed murderer ran loose. That was opposite to the way things should be.

Then again, who said life was fair? Even Christians fell victim to temptation. She should know. Her parents had been prime examples of people who'd talked about how to live a life of faith, yet had failed to do so. Sometimes she wondered if they'd realized how close she'd come to rejecting Jesus because of them. It was only afterward, with the insight of a believer, that she had come to terms with the pain of her past.

And now it seemed she was out of time.

Rising to hands and knees, Sophie labored to regain normal equilibrium. Every breath brought another wave of nausea but each time it seemed to lessen a tiny bit.

"Get up," Carrie ordered. "Stop pretending."

"I'm not pretending. I'm dizzy."

"Good. You'll be less trouble that way." She picked up the flashlight and gestured. "I know you were upstairs when I let myself in with Marlton's key card, so march. We're going back up there."

Sophie would gladly have lunged at her and gone for the gun if she'd been herself. But she wasn't. The images of her surroundings were not only still dim, they vibrated like the shimmer of a mirage on a desert highway.

Nevertheless, she did manage to stand by extending both arms for better balance. Carrie sidled behind her. Prodded her with the gun barrel. "Move it or be shot right here. It's your choice."

Time was what Sophie needed; time to clear her head, time for one of the guards to come to the rescue, or even time for Ryder to finish on the highway and return. She was positive Carrie wouldn't shoot him, even if he confronted her. The rest of them were fair game.

One step at a time, Sophie staggered forward.

Each step brought pain. And the pain caused a rush of adrenaline and made her heart race faster and faster until she wondered if it would pound out of her chest.

"Please, let me rest," she begged the older woman.

"Keep going before I change my mind and give you eternity to rest."

"Why?"

Sophie didn't really want to know what her adversary was thinking, she simply wanted to keep her talking and stall for time. It occurred to her to call to Lily and tell her to hide again, but what good would that do? The converted upstairs apartment was familiar to Carrie as well as having no alternative exits. There was no way Lily could escape. None.

An overwhelming sense of doom pushed Sophie's mind from personal preservation into prayer for Lily. Silently, she pleaded for the child's life.

For Ryder's sake, too, she added. He simply could not lose his only child. *Please, Father. Please help me. Tell me what to do and give me the strength to do it.*

Purposely lagging, Sophie viewed each step as a separate hurdle. This was one race she didn't want to win because the goal at the top of the stairs was Lily. *Dear Jesus!*

Her foot slipped. She went down on one knee,

still grasping the banister. Carrie poked her so hard in the ribs she gasped.

"One more trick like that and you're finished," the murderer warned.

Sophie stayed leaning forward and gained the final landing on her hands and knees. If she could trip Carrie from there, maybe she'd fall backward down the stairs and they'd have a chance to escape.

Unfortunately, Carrie's mind was as alert as Sophie's was hazy, and the plan failed.

"Up," Carrie ordered, circling wide.

Sophie obeyed. Titus knew the other woman from her years as police department secretary and didn't bark. Lily was rubbing her eyes as she sat up and peered through the dimness. "Where's my daddy?"

"We'll see him soon," Carrie said.

What amazed Sophie was how tender Carrie had sounded when speaking to the child. The change in demeanor was startling. And it was frightening because it showed how well she could fake an outward manifestation of kindness.

"I don't suppose you have handcuffs handy," Carrie crooned. "Well, no matter. Lily, go in the closet and bring me a leash."

The child didn't move.

"You heard Mama. Go get a leash."

Seeing how frightened Lily was, Sophie offered to do it. "I can get you one."

"No. The girl needs to learn obedience. She'll get it. Won't you, Lily, dear."

Sophie caught her eye and nodded. "Do as Ms. Carrie says, honey. Please. It's okay."

A slap caught Sophie on the cheek and echoed. She staggered and fell backward into a chair. The moment Carrie said, "Don't interfere," she realized her error. Still, she couldn't let the madwoman abuse the innocent child.

Teary-eyed, Lily returned with a braided leash. "Good girl. Now go sit on the sofa and wait."

All Sophie did this time was give a barely perceptible nod. It was enough to encourage Lily. She perched on the edge of the cushions and petted Titus. He wasn't acting too defensive yet but he was clearly aware that something was wrong.

It took Carrie only seconds to lash Sophie's wrists behind her and tie them to the chair back. Then she went to the sink in the break-room kitchen and filled a glass with tap water. For a moment Sophie thought Carrie might intend kindness. When the woman laid aside the gun to reach into a pocket and produce several pink tablets, she knew better.

Water and pills were offered to Lily. "Here you go, dear. Take these like a good girl."

Lily vigorously shook her head, bringing wrath down on Sophie. "I told you not to spoil her. Now see what you've done."

There was no way Sophie was going to encourage Lily to swallow anything, particularly if it came from Carrie. "You don't have to do that," Sophie said, ducking and cringing when Carrie stomped across the floor and stood before her.

Suddenly, the madwoman wheeled. "Tell you what, Lily," she drawled, sounding half comforting, half menacing, "If you take these pills for Mama I won't shoot your dog."

Lily squealed and threw her arms around Titus's neck. "No! Don't hurt him."

Hand open, Carrie approached. "The pills, or else."

Every time she wasn't being watched, Sophie had struggled to free herself. One more loop and she thought she'd be able to wiggle her left hand out. There! Almost free!

Across the room, a sobbing child was sipping water and weeping as she tried to swallow.

With a final twist and pull, Sophie was loose. She came off the chair with a banshee yell and launched herself at Carrie.

The other woman was taller but less fit. They went down in a jumble of arms and legs. Titus placed himself in front of Lily and began to bark.

Carrie thrashed and kicked away. Sophie tried to hang on to her in spite of the pounding in her injured head and recurring dizziness.

The instant Carrie whirled, Sophie knew why. The gun was back in Carrie's hand. And it was aimed directly at her. All Sophie could do was try to wrest it from her. She gave another guttural shout and charged.

The report of the bullet being fired shook the windows and temporarily made her ears ring.

Shoved backward by the impact she grabbed at her shoulder. There was no pain yet, just a feeling of being punched. Hard.

Incredulous, Sophie stared at the blood flowing between her fingers. Shock softened the blow enough that she could reason, *She shot me. Now how am I going to save Lily?*

Her last thoughts were of Ryder as she closed her eyes and slid to the floor.

Red lights and siren running, the chief slid to a stop in front of the training center. He'd notified dispatch of his actions as he drove. Because of the manpower assigned to the accident he was the first to arrive.

The building was not only pitch-dark, he didn't see Benny Sims guarding the front door.

He drew his sidearm, found the door locked, and tried his key card. The mechanism clicked but the door remained closed tight. Wedged? Maybe. Frustrated, Ryder ran for the rear entrance.

Marlton was lying on the ground there, moaning. Sims was trying to revive him while Phoenix licked both their faces.

Ryder almost lost control and shouted instead of merely asking, "What happened?"

"Don't know," Sims said. "When I woke up I was back here and Dennis was actin' like he is now."

"What about Lily and Sophie?"

The older man looked chagrined. "Sorry, Chief. I can't say."

Ryder burst through the rear door with Phoenix at his heels. The flashlight on his belt was all he needed to follow the dog when he picked up a scent. This time, there was no hesitation. Phoenix bounded up the stairs so fast it looked as if his paws never touched the ground.

Breathless, Ryder caught up and played the light over the room. Phoenix had gone straight to a figure on the floor and was nudging it with his nose.

"Sophie!"

Ryder's heart nearly stopped. Pushing the concerned canine aside, he knelt at her side and touched her neck, looking for a carotid pulse. Tears of relief blurred his vision when he found one. It was strong.

He grabbed his radio and called for an ambulance, then gently rolled her over. There was a lot of blood on her shoulder but it wasn't pulsing. "Praise God." Whoever had shot Sophie had missed the subclavian artery. She had a chance.

It took only seconds to locate a small kitchen towel and press it over the entry wound. He put a second towel behind her shoulder where the bullet had exited leaving more damage.

His hands were shaking. "Sophie? Sophie, can you hear me?" There was no reply but he did think he sensed slight movement. "Hold still, honey. You've been shot. An ambulance is on the way."

Her lips moved. Ryder leaned closer.

"Lily…"

Ashen faced and barely able to think straight, he listened closely. When Sophie started to go limp again, he begged, "What about Lily?"

The hazel eyes he loved so dearly opened. Lashes fluttered. Tears gathered. "Carrie."

"Carrie was here? She's the one who shot you?"

Sophie licked her dry lips and tried to nod, groaning in pain instead.

"Lie still. It won't be long now," Ryder said as his heart shattered into a million fragments. Carrie had his little girl. Unless he got her back, life for him was over.

Gazing down at Sophie he added, *I need her, too*, and bent to place a tender kiss on her forehead.

Her pale skin felt icy, clammy with shock and loss of blood. If he hadn't known better he'd have pulled her into his arms and cradled her. The smartest thing he could do, however, was continue to slow the bleeding and pray that he'd have the chance to show her how much he cared after she healed.

She had to be all right, Ryder insisted. She simply had to be.

He spent a moment praying for her recovery, then leaned over again and kissed her lips, following with a whispered, "I love you."

Sophie drifted in and out of consciousness, happier when her dreams brought peace than when reality carried suffering. Somewhere, in the midst of all that, she sensed Ryder's presence, felt him touching her cheek. That was wonderful until she recalled bits and pieces of what had happened to Lily.

Strong hands held her down as she struggled to rise. "I—I have to go…"

"To the hospital," a paramedic said. "You've lost a lot of blood."

Behind that man she saw the blurry face of her dreams. "Ryder!"

He grasped her free hand. "I'm here. You're going to be all right once a doctor patches you up."

"No, I have to go after Lily."

"What happened? Can you tell me more?"

"Carrie was here. She took Lily."

"Did you see them leave?"

"No." Sophie sighed. "But she made Lily take pills. I tried to…to stop it."

Another medic urged Ryder to back off. "We've given her a shot for the pain. She won't be talking much longer. Let us load her so we can come back for the other guys."

"Is that when Carrie shot you?" Ryder asked. Sophie saw him brace himself to keep from being pushed away as she was lifted onto a wheeled gurney.

"Yes." Tears welled. "I'm so sorry."

"We'll find them," he promised.

She wanted to offer to go with him, to rise from the thin mattress and strike back. Instead, she sensed movement and heard men talking as they strapped her down before carrying her downstairs and pushing her out onto the sidewalk.

Bright, flashing lights hurt her eyes so she shut them and felt teardrops trickling down her temples. Where was Ryder? Was he going to come with her? To look after her?

A niggling fear lingered in the back of her mind as she succumbed to the effects of the narcotics. Something else was wrong, wasn't it? Something terrible.

Sophie fought to remember. It was important. Her thoughts cried out for Ryder. He would know. He would fix it.

Colors blinked at the edges of her closed eyes. A vortex of sound enveloped her with mechanical beeps and internal heartbeats and the wail of a siren.

Then, everything vanished, including her pain.

NINETEEN

Ryder gave the K-9 rookies their orders via radio. Some had to come from the accident scene and pick up their dogs. Others, like Whitney Godwin and Ellen Foxcroft, had not responded to the wreck and were a little closer.

Protocol insisted Ryder must wait for backup. His heart disagreed. Breaking the rules he'd been hired to enforce would set a bad example but he didn't care. This was Lily he was tracking.

Checking Titus, he realized that the old dog was already moving as if he was hurt, so he had no choice but to use Phoenix. Once the younger dog was in his working harness he stopped jumping around.

The sweater they had used for Phoenix's tracking test was gone, but Lily's sandals had been left behind. Ryder picked them up, stuck one in his pocket, and led his new K-9 partner out into the street.

"Sit." When he held out the small sandal for

the dog to smell, the sight of it tied his gut in knots. "Seek."

One more quick sniff and Phoenix was off. He started down the sidewalk toward the police station, then stopped, circled and took off across the street.

Ryder gave him his head, slowing him only enough to keep pace. He didn't dare release the dog and chance losing sight of him.

Phoenix strained against the restraint, pulling as if his life depended upon it. Ryder could totally identify. He, too, was pushing to the edge of his endurance.

Up and down curbs, around trees and away from town they went. The best part about the long run was that Carrie hadn't gotten into a car and driven away, leaving no discernible trail. If she had, there was no way any K-9, no matter how special, could have successfully tracked her.

Bristling and panting, Phoenix slowed. His nose checked the ground, then the air. They had come to one of the abandoned houses that had yet to be torn down or repaired as part of a Desert Valley beautification project.

Ryder ducked behind an overflowing trash Dumpster next to the ramshackle building and listened. Phoenix was making no effort to go on, nor did he seem confused.

As far as the dog was concerned, he'd done his job. He'd found Lily. All that was left was for

Ryder to radio his position, which he immediately did, then figure out how to gain access to the house without being seen.

He circled to the rear with his K-9 partner at his side, pulling him back just in time to keep him from scratching on the door. "Sit." It was more a hiss than a command. He could tell that Phoenix was agitated. That was nothing compared to how Ryder felt. He was ready to smash his way in and tear Carrie Dunleavy limb from limb.

It took a series of deep breaths for him to regain emotional control. When he was sure he was ready, he slowly twisted the knob on the back door.

It turned easily.

A beam of light illuminated the face of a child stretched out on the kitchen table. Lily's face. And Carrie was standing next to her, stroking her blond hair as the child yawned. It was hard for Ryder to reconcile the mousy woman in front of him with the cold-blooded murderer he knew her to be— until he looked into her eyes and saw wickedness gleaming. She was every bit as evil to the core as he'd imagined.

"What took you so long," Carrie asked with a smirk. "One of my cats could have found us sooner than that miserable excuse for a search and rescue dog." She gave a maniacal laugh. "Too bad your old dog was out of commission right when you needed him."

"How did you know that?" He'd entered and closed the door behind him, isolating Phoenix to keep him from attacking Carrie and getting in the way. When Ryder made his move to disarm her, he didn't want to have to worry about the dog.

"Titus gave me trouble, just like I knew he would, so I kicked him in the ribs. Not too hard, mind you. Just enough to slow him down."

"What about Lily? What did you give her?"

"I don't know what you mean."

"Yes, you do. You made her swallow pills."

"Just cold pills." She frowned. "How did you know about that?

"Sophie saw you do it."

Carrie cursed, high and screeching. "She's still alive? I thought for sure I'd finished her." She eyed Lily. "Oh, well, at least that woman is out of the way and we can bring our perfect family together as it was meant to be."

Ryder didn't know what to say. Carrie obviously thought of the three of them as a family. He couldn't imagine anything more loathsome. Nevertheless, he began to build on her fantasy. "You wanted me and now you have me. We don't need Lily."

"Should I kill her, then?"

"No!"

"Humph. That's what I thought. We need our little girl to make a real family."

"Right, right." Ryder holstered his gun and

raised his hands partway. "See? I'm unarmed. You don't need that gun, either. We're all friends here."

As the woman studied him, he hoped and prayed his expression masked his true feelings. Truth to tell, if he got his hands on her, the person who had taken one love from him and was threatening to take more, he wondered if he'd be able to do his duty instead of following the urge for retribution.

Instincts for revenge were strong, but his faith was stronger, although it fluctuated from moment to moment. If he had returned to the training center and found Sophie dead instead of merely wounded, he wasn't sure he'd have been able to control himself—then or now.

Carrie smiled. "We are friends, aren't we? It was such a thrill to see you enjoy my cooking when I brought treats to the station."

It took all the self-control Ryder could muster to keep from gagging at the thought. For five years he had treated his wife's killer as an equal, a friend and coworker. What a fool he'd been! They all had. And how convincing a true sociopath like Carrie could be.

"You—you can cook for me a lot from now on," he said. Sidelong peeks at Lily showed him her breathing was steady and deep.

"As a good wife should. That was another reason Melanie was all wrong for you. She hated to cook. You were practically wasting away while she was pregnant."

Fists clenched behind his back, Ryder gritted his teeth. He had to take this, to go along with her fantasies long enough to gain the upper hand. If Carrie even suspected how much he hated her, there was no telling what she'd do.

Something inside of him countered the feelings of revulsion with a reminder that even Carrie was redeemable in the sight of God. He disagreed mightily. No one that evil was worth saving.

You're wrong, Ryder's conscience insisted. *Hate will consume you like a fire, leaving nothing but ashes.*

There was no way he was going to be able to instantly change his mind and find a way to forgive Carrie for all she'd done. Not without a lot of prayer and soul-searching, first. But maybe he could at least talk to her, stall for time until the rest of the rookies arrived.

"I put my gun away. How about you putting yours down, too?" Ryder suggested again.

"You'll be nice?"

"Of course. Haven't I always been nice to you, Carrie?"

She tucked the revolver in her pocket. "You never took me to the dance. I wanted to go every year and you never asked me. Nobody did."

"Is that what disappointed you about Brian and

Mike?" The blond rookies who were like stand-ins for him in Carrie's mind.

"Well, duh. Of course. It was partly my fault. They had the same hair color and blue eyes as you do but they were poor substitutes. I should have been more patient."

"And waited for the right man," Ryder offered.

Carrie smiled sweetly. "Yes. For you. I didn't think you'd ever get over the loss of your Melanie until I saw how you were treating Sophie. I gave up too soon, that's all. God was going to bring us together. I just needed to get some of the obstacles out of the way."

"If you really believe in God," Ryder said, "why would you act as if you're smarter than He is and separate a man from his wife?"

The sweet smile vanished. "You aren't listening. I told you. She was all wrong for you. You need to be with me." She gazed at the sleeping child. "And our little girl."

"But what bothered you about Veronica Earnshaw?" Ryder asked. "She and I had a professional relationship. That was all."

Carrie's brown eyes hardened even more behind her large glasses. "Veronica caught me staring at James Harrison, the next blond rookie that reminded me of you. She made fun of me. She even winked at me. And then she told James she'd come over to his room at the rookies' condo to give him and his dog a private training refresher.

Private! I knew what that meant. James was mine. Mine! He was always so nice to me. He even said he would have asked me to the police dance if he didn't have to go on a stakeout to try to catch Veronica's killer." She laughed.

Ryder felt sick.

"Isn't that funny?" Carrie asked. "I'm glad James didn't disappoint me like the others."

Harrison had no idea how close he'd come to being killed, Ryder realized.

"And Marian Foxcroft?" Ryder asked. "How did she disappoint you?"

"That rich snob got a little too close to finding me out," Carrie said, shaking her head. "Nosy old woman."

"All right," Ryder managed to choke out. "Now I understand everything that's happened. Give me a hug and let's make up."

"Can I trust you?" She was eyeing him with suspicion and edging away as he tried to work his way close enough to grab and disarm her.

Smiling, he reached out to her. The instant she made her decision he saw it in her face. The wrinkles and frown lines relaxed. She circled the table.

"I want a kiss," Carrie said, giving him a dreamy look. "I've waited a long, long time."

Ryder grasped her wrists to keep her from going for the gun in her pocket, spun her around and snapped handcuffs on her before he relieved her of the weapon.

Screaming and cursing, Carrie reverted to the insanity that controlled her while Ryder reported by radio.

"We're ready to breach," Tristan McKeller reported.

"You won't have to. Come take custody of my prisoner," Ryder said. "And call another ambulance. My daughter needs to go to the hospital."

"I'm fine," Sophie kept arguing.

The two nurses who had been assigned to keep her quiet until they could transfer her to a regular room were taking their jobs seriously. "You've lost too much blood. You'll need a couple of days' rest before you'll be ready for discharge, let alone go back to work."

"You don't understand. They need me out there. I train search and rescue dogs."

"If they're already trained, they should work without you, right?"

"It's complicated."

"And you're stubborn," the darker-haired nurse said. "I've had some cantankerous patients in my thirty years of nursing but you take the cake."

"What did you do with my clothes?" Sophie asked, looking around the cubicle. "I don't see them."

Younger and with spiked red hair, the other RN patted Sophie's free hand. "We had to bag them for the cops because this was a crime. Trust me, you're going to want to burn them. They'll never come clean."

"Can I at least have something to put on besides this thin gown. I'm freezing."

"I'll get you a warm blanket," the first nurse said. She eyed her coworker. "You can give her some scrubs if you like. She's not going anywhere barefoot."

Smiling, Sophie thought, *Oh, yeah? Watch me.*

Riding in the ambulance with Lily, Ryder kept trying to wake her and succeeded in getting a few mumbled responses. Two medics were monitoring her respiration and blood pressure.

"She'll be fine in no time," one assured him. "They'll want to do a blood test in the ER to make sure she wasn't given anything stronger than cold pills. It's just a precaution. Her vitals are good. I wouldn't worry."

Ryder was dubious. Carrie had sworn she hadn't given the child anything dangerous, but he wasn't about to take her home without a thorough checkup. Besides, he needed to see Sophie. To tell her Lily had been found and Carrie arrested.

"Were you the crew that picked up a gunshot victim at the Canyon County Training Center tonight?" he asked.

"Yeah. We dropped her at the hospital."

"Do you think she'll still be there?"

The paramedic draped his stethoscope around

his neck and smiled. "I doubt they had to send her on if that's what you mean."

"Thanks."

"She one of yours, Chief?"

Ryder knew the man meant professionally. His answer was far from it. He smiled as he continued to hold Lily's hand. "Yes. She's definitely one of mine."

Getting the hospital garb on over her bandaged shoulder was painful. Sophie managed with the help of the red-haired nurse. By the time she was dressed she was breathing hard and perspiring. "Whew! That was not fun. I need a minute to catch my breath."

"Take all the time you need. I'll be back to check on you soon. Your warm blanket is right here if you want it."

"I'm good for now. Thanks."

"We're short on rooms due to the big accident."

"I'm so sorry. I should have asked. Were there a lot of serious injuries?"

"The worst victims were flown to Flagstaff so I can't really say. Ours are stable."

"Thank God. Literally," Sophie said.

"You've got that right. Do you want me to help you put your feet up so you can lie down here?"

"No. Thanks. I just want to sit for a few minutes and let the pain subside." That much was true. What Sophie did not say was that she hoped to be able to slip easily to the floor and walk, despite her condition.

She had no plans beyond that. First, she had to prove to herself that she was ambulatory. Then she'd find a way to rejoin Ryder and Lily, wherever they were.

That was the only goal that mattered. She had to know they were both all right. That Carrie had not killed them.

Her stomach knotted and she doubled over, almost losing her balance. The image of Lily, swallowing pills to protect Titus from harm, was one she would never forget.

All Sophie knew at this point was that Carrie had wanted to make Lily her own daughter. To do that, she either had to marry Ryder or get him out of the way and kidnap the child. Either could have happened while Sophie lay unconscious and bleeding.

Something vague kept drifting through her mind. It concerned Ryder and triggered tender feelings—the kind she'd been having for him since he'd first embraced her in innocence.

"Lord, help me do this," she whispered. Using her good arm, she pushed off the edge of the bed. The landing was soft, yet jarred her shoulder enough to send a wave of pain and nausea through her.

Deep breathing helped. She let go of the bed.

Stood straight and determined. Took one step, then another.

She was halfway to the exit when she saw Ryder. He was accompanying a wheeled gurney and holding Lily's hand. The child was stirring!

Sophie gasped. Her pulse sped. Pain vanished. Ryder looked up and recognized her. The love in his expression was so overwhelming she couldn't move.

In seconds he was beside her, his arm around her waist.

She sagged against him, drawing on his strength. "Is Lily...?"

"She's fine. Just sleepy."

"I was afraid."

"I know. So was I. But it's over now."

"You got Carrie?"

"Handcuffed and hauled off to jail," Ryder assured her. "Are you okay?"

"I am now that you're here."

Relief swept through Sophie. She began to collapse, and he caught her up, taking care not to bump her injured shoulder.

"Do you remember much?" he asked.

"Not a lot after Carrie shot me. Lily was very brave."

"I get the idea you were, too."

She snuggled closer and laid her head on his chest. "I had to try to save her."

"I know." They were keeping pace with the gurney where the little girl dozed. "Do you remember anything about the time when I found you?"

"Not really. I've tried, but all I get is warm feelings."

"You're on the right track," Ryder said tenderly. "I was so worried when I saw you lying there, bleeding, I couldn't help myself. I told you I loved you."

Sophie lifted her head to smile up at him. "You did?"

"Uh-huh."

"I don't remember." The smile grew to a grin despite the throbbing pain of her wound. "Maybe you'd better say it again."

"Gladly." He paused to tenderly kiss her forehead. "I love you, Sophie."

She was fighting back tears of joy when she replied, "I love you, too.

Lily skipped into Sophie's hospital room and presented a bouquet of wildflowers that were more seeds and insects and broken stems than blossoms. Sophie had never received such a beautiful gift.

"Thank you," she said, taking the flowers with a wide grin and misty eyes.

"I picked them myself," Lily announced.

Ryder backed her up. "That, she did. I offered to buy some for her to give you but she had to do it herself. Reminds me of you."

"I just did what was necessary," Sophie said quietly, watching the little girl begin to play with an arrangement of get well cards on a side table. "They say I can get out of here this afternoon. Will you be available to give me a lift home?"

He perched on the edge of her bed and clasped her hand. "I will give you anything and everything you want, if you'll let me."

Sophie smiled. "I have all I need as long as the two of you are around." She arched a brow. "Well, except for a dog or two. Life isn't complete without furry friends."

"That's what Lily says. She wants a puppy, too, now that Titus doesn't want to play."

"He's healing okay?" Sophie asked, sobering. "I can't believe Carrie kicked him."

"Tanya says he'll be fine. Which reminds me," Ryder said. "Ellen's mother is awake and talking. Marian even remembers when Carrie knocked her out, which is another surprise. And another charge to add to the indictment, not that we need it to send Carrie away for keeps."

Sophie's heart swelled with thankfulness. "That's wonderful. Poor Marian. I was afraid the coma would last the rest of her life."

"I think we all wondered, despite plenty of prayers on her behalf."

"What happens now? I guess all the rookies will be reassigned now that the murders are solved. There's no way your budget can pay all those wages, is there?"

"Normally, no, but we're working on that." Ryder was stroking the back of her hand with his thumb. "Louise has already submitted her retirement paperwork and is helping Harmon and Marlton with theirs. I'll have at least three openings. Four, if you count Ken Buck's conviction for lying under oath and evidence tampering. I'm hoping I can convince four of the rookies to stay on permanently."

"Then only one rookie can't stay if they want to?" Sophie was so excited about the prospect she was almost giddy.

"If that's what they decide, probably," Ryder said. "James Harrison wanted to return to Wyoming, but unless Madison Coles can get a reporter's job up there he won't go. Tristan's happy because his sister, Mia, is staying out of trouble here. Besides, he's marrying Ariel and she has a teaching job to go back to as soon as her maternity leave is over."

"What about Whitney and the doctor? Evans took over management of the clinic and it's thriving. Surely he'll want to stay after he passes his licensing exams, so she will, too."

Ryder was smiling and nodding. "That's what I'd hope."

Sophie was counting silently. "That only leaves Shane and Gina, right? I wonder if I can convince her to stay on with me. She's a great asset to the training program."

"Don't forget Ellen Foxcroft," Ryder reminded her.

"It never dawned on me that she'd leave Desert Valley. Not now that her mother is recovering and she has the assistance dog center up and flourishing. With Lee Earnshaw going back to vet school, I suppose she might want to be closer to him, though."

"A little distance won't bother their romance," Ryder assured her. "Lee plans to commute on weekends as much as possible. With Ellen's money they won't have any hardship traveling back and forth."

Sighing, Sophie relaxed back against the elevated pillows. "Then they're all happy. My whole rookie class is taken care of."

He smiled in response. "I just realized something—all five rookies can stay if they choose to. Now that I'm the chief, my old spot is open too. That makes five. Now all we have to consider is us."

"Us? As in you and me?" Sophie eyed Lily. "Let's not rush things, okay? I want our marriage to be a joy for everybody, not just you and me." She detected a mischievous twinkle in Ryder's loving gaze. "What?"

"I don't recall asking you to marry me, that's all."

"You will," Sophie told him with a wry smile.

"Oh? What if I don't?"

Sitting up with a slight wince when her shoulder hurt, she reached to slip her other hand around his neck and pull him closer. "If you wait too long, then I will be forced to ask you, instead. I don't care who pops the question as long as the mutual answer is *yes*."

"Yes." Ryder whispered it against her lips just before he kissed her. "How about a Christmas wedding?"

"I prefer Valentine's Day," Sophie said. "But we certainly should plan to spend Christmas together. That will give me a chance to win Lily over. I can help her participate in the church Christmas pageant, for one thing."

Ryder laughed. "She told me last year that she wasn't going to be in that play again unless she got to be Mary and carry the baby doll, so you may have your hands full."

Sophie joined him with a soft chuckle as they both watched the little girl playing with the greeting cards. "I don't doubt that a bit," Sophie said. "I can hardly wait."

EPILOGUE

Spring spread an abundance of wildflowers across the desert, as if preparing the entire countryside for the nuptials of Sophie Williams and Ryder Hayes.

The yard of the Desert Valley Community Church was bedecked with the same kind of floral decorations, in keeping with the wishes of a certain little blonde girl who had scattered petals down the aisle between rows of folding chairs for her mother-to-be and matron of honor, Gina Weston. Gina's husband, Shane, was Ryder's best man.

Nervous—in a good way—Sophie paused to appreciate the wide blue sky, breathe pure desert air and thank the Lord for this day. Every member of last year's rookie class had married and all were in attendance, including their working dogs. Titus had accompanied Lily, carrying her basket of flower petals down the aisle for her and garnering broad grins.

With Phoenix at her side, Sophie smoothed her simple white sheath and grasped her bouquet. Lily had so admired the floral crown that held Sophie's veil she had fastened flowers to the dog's harness, making him strongly resemble a half-finished parade float.

The wind ruffled her veil. Sophie heard the music that was her cue and started toward the altar.

There was Ryder! She had asked him to wear his uniform instead of a tuxedo and he was so handsome he took her breath away.

Each step brought her closer to him, closer to the happiness she had long believed to be out of her reach, closer to a real home. A home she had almost lost before she'd had a chance to discover the possibility.

She passed her bouquet and the end of Phoenix's leash to Gina as she took Ryder's hand.

"Dearly Beloved," the pastor began.

Too soon it was over. Sophie knew she'd participated in the entire ceremony but her brain had yet to process the details. Everything was too wonderful. Too amazing. Too extraordinary to be real.

Lily tugged on her arm. "Can I hold your flowers?"

"All right. But you have to give them back later so take really good care of them, okay?"

"Okay." Her wide blue eyes looked up at her father. "Now?" she asked.

Ryder nodded. "Yes, now."

The child pulled to urge Sophie to bend down, wrapped her arms around her neck and said, "I love you... Mommy," then skipped off carrying the bridal bouquet.

Sophie was blinking back happy tears. When she looked at her new husband, his eyes were suspiciously sparkling, too. "You rehearsed that?"

"Not exactly. She kept pestering me about calling you Mommy and I told her to wait until it was official."

"She wanted to do it before? When?"

Ryder shrugged. "I don't remember. Probably around the time when the two of you Magi were leading dogs dressed as camels to Bethlehem in the Christmas pageant."

"And all this time I thought she was having trouble accepting me as her mother." Sophie made a silly face. "If I still had my flowers I'd be tempted to smack you with them for making us wait."

Laughing, he pulled his bride into his arms and kissed her again. And again.

Whoops and catcalls echoed in the balmy afternoon air. Someone hollered, "Hey, you gonna serve this or should we let the dogs loose?"

"I told you that second cake would be a problem," Ryder said. "Some of our rowdiest guests are animals. Real ones."

Sophie agreed. "Normal wedding cake is bad

for them. I was just trying to make everybody feel welcome."

She kept hold of Ryder's hand as they approached the refreshment table. A three tiered wedding cake with white frosting and piped floral decorations stood at one end of the display, as expected.

At the other end was Sophie's answer to their canine guests. It was by far the most popular offering, particularly to the four-legged attendees. Liver paste was the glue that held row after row of crunchy, colored, dog treats to the sides of a pyramid almost as high as the real wedding cake.

Ryder laughed and looked at his team—all of whom had decided to stay on in Desert Valley. With six months under their belt on a twisty murder investigation, they were well on their way to moving from rookies to seasoned police officers.

And through it all, each one of them had found love. Shane and Gina. Whitney and David. Ellen and Lee. James and Madison. Tristan and Ariel.

Himself and Sophie. Six months ago, he and Sophie had barely been on speaking terms. Now they were husband and wife.

He thought—for just a moment—of the insane woman who'd started them all down these unexpected paths. Former Desert Valley Police Department secretary Carrie Dunleavy had been quickly convicted of the murders of his late wife, Melanie Hayes, rookies Brian Miller and Mike Riverton, and lead dog trainer Veronica Earnshaw—and attempted murder of Marian Foxcroft. All thanks to her confession and guilty plea. She would be in prison for the rest of her life.

Ryder took his mind off the past and focused on the present—and his future. He took his new bride's hand and they stepped behind the dog-treat cake. Cameras and cell phones flashed.

"Together?" she asked.

"Absolutely. But if you make me taste that stuff I won't be happy."

"I'd never waste good liver on a man," Sophie teased. She plucked several treats from the top of the "cake" and Ryder did the same.

Before throwing them to the waiting dogs she called out, "Sit."

Every dog and half the guests obeyed as if the move had been rehearsed. One look at Ryder's smug expression told her it had.

"Are you going to keep surprising me for the rest of my life?" she joked, trying to make herself understood while laughing so hard that tears were streaming down her face.

"That's the plan," he said through his own laughter. "Are you ready?"

"Oh, yes."

Sophie proved it by wrapping her arms around his neck and kissing him soundly—before leaning back to dab a tiny spot of pâté on the tip of his nose.

Cameras flashed again. That was going to make a great picture to show their grandchildren someday.

* * * * *

If you liked the ROOKIE K-9 UNIT *series,*
keep an eye out for
ROOKIE K-9 UNIT CHRISTMAS
by Lenora Worth and Valerie Hansen
releasing November 2016.

Dear Reader,

I am in love with these K-9 cops and their handlers. Every one is special, just as every real dog and person is unique. I think we make a mistake when we expect the same from each individual, as with Ryder wanting Phoenix to be just like Titus.

When we experience a catastrophic loss the way Ryder Hayes did in this ongoing story, we need to come to terms with the fact that nothing will ever be the same. Trying to force another person into the same role will fail because no two people are alike. We change, too, as time passes. We can't go back. But we can go forward, knowing that God is with us and Jesus loves us. It's simple and complicated at the same time. Just trust in the newness of tomorrow.

Blessings,
Valerie Hansen

REQUEST YOUR FREE BOOKS!
2 FREE WHOLESOME ROMANCE NOVELS IN LARGER PRINT
PLUS 2
FREE
MYSTERY GIFTS

WESTERN WP PROMISES

WPBPA16R